Buried Dreams

Buried Dreams

Chas Silvester

'Buried Dreams'

RedSox
Press

Published by RedSox Press 2020
www.redsoxpress.co.uk

ISBN 978-1-9161234-2-7

A catalogue record for this book is available from
the British Library

RedSox Press Limited Reg. No. 09863441

'Buried Dreams' is dedicated to:

Sue and Sean White, who have put up with me for many years, particularly during lockdown.

My father, Norman White, who conked out in February 2020 having got whiff of trouble ahead.

To all the wonderful people at The Solihull Lodge Writing Group, particularly our leader Matt Nunn, and everyone else who have been a continual source of inspiration and humour.

Scott Brown who has a similar sense of the absurd and has given me confidence to perform in public at Poetry Bites, Happy Heart and other venues around Birmingham daft enough to give us both air time.

To Birmingham Walking Footballers, Gloucester City and Birmingham City, keep right on!

CHAS SILVESTER lived in Sheffield from 1977 to 1981 and spent the most of his time watching local bands and football.

Has spent much of his life travelling and his present whereabouts are unknown. In his more lucid moments he claimed to be a traveller in time having originated in Gloucester in 1877 named Tom White existing under a number of aliases including Chas Silvester and served a number of prison sentences for fraud and deception until disappearing from a locked cell at Gloucester Prison in 1900 and never being heard of again.

Prologue: 2070

It is 2070, and The Earth is on its last knockings ravaged by the stupidity of humans who have contributed to the devastation of the planet. Temperatures have risen to such levels that many areas of the planet are uninhabitable and the remainder is either flooded or permanently in drought.

England has been reduced to a handful of communities based around the larger cities. The inhabitants live to work and work to live, labouring in factories to produce components for the construction of the transport for the elite rulers of the metropolises. The ordinary people live an almost mediaeval existence with basic entertainments to distract them from their everyday drudgery.

No one, apart from the ruling establishment is allowed to leave the confines of their metropolis, and education for the majority of the population is basic with all books, films, music, historical records deleted or destroyed. The majority of the population do not know anything about life outside their immediate environment and are certainly not aware of the finite time that the Earth has left to exist.

Steel City comprises the remnants of the city of Sheffield with a transport system connecting living, working, and leisure facilities with no one being able to survive in the open air for more than short periods due to the high temperature. Living and working conditions are brutal with control being kept by a harsh, uncaring, draconian establishment largely made up of representatives from the Sovok Republic who oversee England.

The Sovok Republic have generally lost interest in exploiting the resources of England and are planning to scale back their involvement and leave the locals to their fate.

MAP

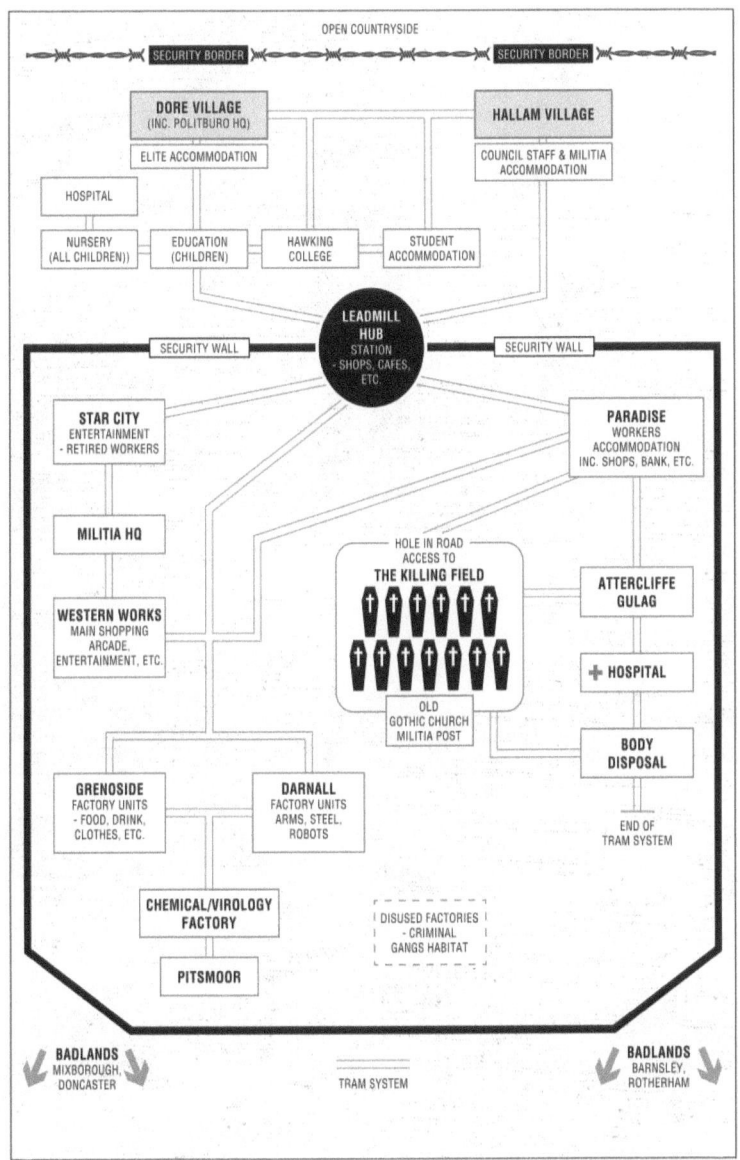

PART ONE: DISCONTENTMENT

CHAPTER ONE

Ashton Lukashenko checked behind him to make sure he was not being followed, he checked the number of the living pod again and made his way along a dark and draughty corridor. The only sound was the clanky air conditioning. He stopped at *corok chityre* (44) and activated his commtel device to announce his arrival. The security door slid open and he stepped inside. Ashton looked around and saw who he assumed was Veronica Franco standing by a screen showing panoramic views of long-gone snowfields. Looking forward to this illicit liaison he strutted towards Veronica. Suddenly he was hit from behind with an electric stun weapon and he sunk to the floor as two masked figures secured him with an electronic force field. They removed their face coverings and smirked at each other. "Let therevenge start."

CHAPTER TWO

Adi Newton was in historical terms a *gumshoe* but liked to advertise himself on the *Dark Net* as a Cybernet Investigation Detective or CYD. Adi aka Cyd worked on the edges and in the cracks of society. He prided himself on achieving resolution and at times revenge for wronged members of the mixed and diverse population of the Greater Metropolis of Steel City which before 'The Heat Attack of 2043' had been called Sheffield.

Adi aka Cyd was a tall, lithe man with a shaved head and a prominent scar running from his left ear to the corner of his mouth. On the other side of his face were a dagger tattoo and diamond hoops in his eyebrow. Adi rarely smiled and always had a serious look on his dark-skinned face as if something was continually weighing on his mind.

Cyd as he was known by the netherworld of the Steel City, was a Hawking or genius of the web. He had graduated with the highest honours from Steel City International Symposium for Cybernautics, also known colloquially as Hawking College.

Cyd was smart and had found ways of bypassing the 'healthy life' chip. This was installed in the brains of children who passed the SATs examination and virtual gaming test at the age of seven, which identified their future career path and allowed them to live in the elite Hallam village. The young Adi had passed with flying colours and had been fast-tracked into the Corporation which administered the city. Adi had found a way to negate the effects of the chip which inhibited the individual from taking drugs and using alcohol which had been prohibited many years previously. Adi had not been frightened of venturing outside of the elite areas and had visited cyber speakeasies taking drugs, drinking illicit moonshine and engaging in extreme video roleplay with other 'disenchanteds' from all over the cybersphere.

Adi had discovered a cache of music from nearly a hundred years ago. In the absence of any current and recent music, he had an extensive collection of tracks from the 1970s and had distributed it to many like-minded individuals. The only music available was through official channels and consisted of electronic dirges which were designed to boost production in the factories. Adi was an expert on life in Steel City in the 1970s and had studied some old transcripts of concerts and people talking during the period and often wished he was able to transport himself back in time away from the current miserable times.

The senior levels of the Corporation that ran the metropolis were not tolerant of Adi and similar malcontents who were free-thinkers and were determined to block their progress into the elite echelons of society. They exiled them to live in the run-down high-rise flats that surrounded the Metropolis where the plastic waste was ankle-deep, and the heat outside was only bearable for short periods.

The high-rise accommodation at Paradise was full of people who worked in the factory areas of Steel City on subsistence wages with no health and safety precautions or rights. The flats were run down and essential services rationed with water and heating only available at certain times. The only constant was the video screen installed in each living area that pumped out information and propaganda from the Steel City Positive News channel.

The workers would travel to one of the remaining four areas of Steel City to work. Attercliffe was the site of Steel City Gulag and the Wednesday

Hospital. Grenoside housed the metal manufacturing factories that provided repairs for the transport system and weapons for the Corporation militia. Darnell was where the food establishments were based, providing the sustenance to keep everyone in Steel City nourished to a basic level and able to work. There were restricted areas with factories that produced goods for the elite areas of Hallam Village and Dore for export to the Sovok Republic. There were also areas where children were raised and educated by the state and retirement accommodation for those lucky enough to live long enough.

Everything was self-contained, and only members of the ruling politburo were ever allowed to set out outside the confines of the metropolis of Steel City.

The remaining area of employment was The Western Works, where there were colossal Corporation approved entertainment complexes as well as official food, drink and clothing markets. There were many other unofficial vendors across the city selling all manner of goods and services. The other area that was in use was The Farm at Heeley entered through 'Tut Ole in Road' portal which led to The Killing Field. Beyond the living and working areas of Steel City was the Badlands towards Barnsley and

Rotherham where nothing lived due to the poisonous atmosphere.

CHAPTER THREE

Adi was in his work pod in The Western Works surrounded by electronic equipment; his main credit-earning occupation was targeting ransomware cyber malcontents. They would attempt to gain access to personal accounts to divert their credit savings to off-world accounts and send the time-honoured message, "I've encrypted your files, pay me, or they will be gone forever." Adi would track these cyber crooks down and give their details to the internal Revenge and Retribution team who would eliminate them.

Adi was humming along to his favourite Clock DVA music, which he had illegally downloaded from an obsolete website, as he tried to crack a difficult computer code when his security system growled as a hologram appeared in front of him. Adi recognised the form of Woodward, the Head of Revenge and Retribution for the Corporation. Even though Adi had been banished from the elite area of Steel City, they still recognised his unique skills and technological abilities. They would hire him for clandestine and off the radar investigations and allowed him to rent an office and living quarters in the more upmarket area of the city.

Woodward spoke with a robotic drawl, "Felicitations Citizen Newton, we have a new task for you, it is vitally important, and we will double your usual recompense. Of course, you have no choice for your co-operation. We will send the usual encrypted file with details and instructions and strict deadline."

Adi wondered if Woodward really existed and not just a technological invention of the elite imperial class. However, he knew he had no choice to get on with it and mentally clicked the file on the screen. He opened the memory bank in his brain, and the encryption code appeared on the front of the file and on all the screens around the room. Adi had been ordered to make his way to The Killing Field where he would be met and directed to a personal meeting with Woodward. This intrigued Adi, as all previous dealings had been completed electronically.

CHAPTER FOUR

Adi made his way through the disused shopping centre between The Western Works and Heeley with jets of steam escaping from the drains clogged up with plastic rubbish. Adi had his protective cap on to deflect the rays of the ferocious sun which could cause instant burns on exposed skin as he dodged between the buildings. Adi turned the corner by the memorial to the Crucible Snooker Club destroyed by the Anti-Brexit Liberation Army cyber terrorists in their campaign of destruction many years previously. This movement had ended when most of Europa was made uninhabitable during the clash of the EU army and the reformed Socialist Sovok Republic over Ukrainye. The EU mandarins foolishly called their bluff regarding the use of their Megatron nuclear fission device. The United Kingdom, or what was left of it, finally ended up trying to re-join Europa at the point it ceased to exist.

Adi was confronted suddenly by two figures in official red and white protective suits. These were the security workers who worked for The Revenge and

Retribution squad and ruthlessly completed the tasks they were given

They set off with Adi following, picking their way through the alleys clogged with plastic debris until they suddenly reached The Killing Field and the sight laid before him chilled his whole body despite the fierce cauldron of heat.

This was the punishment field for those who transgressed against the metropolis of Steel City. Row on row of metal crosses with the charred remains of criminals, political activists, intellectuals and the losers from life or death reality net shows. The unfortunate victims were left to char in the sun while the microchips injected into their bodies simultaneously burnt them up from the inside. These executions were live-streamed to deter citizens from becoming the next candidates for heat crucifixion.

The two figures suddenly dived into what looked like a boarded-up worship hall. All religion was banned many years previously, although some of the buildings remained. A shutter swung upwards allowing the guides to duck down and enter, Adi scrambled on the rough ground to follow and just made it through as the entrance slammed shut. Adi was lying face down and struggled to his feet in the cramped space, he looked up, expecting to see his guides, but they had disappeared. He tried to get back out the door, but he could see nothing except smooth reinforced steel with no apparent edges or joins.

Suddenly, the room filled with a blinding light, and a rectangular screen appeared on the wall. A balaclava-clad face appeared, and the staring blue eyes scanned Adi up and down. Adi went to speak, but a crushing noise emanated from the four corners of the room with lights flashing in time with the music.

Adi fell to his knees as the throbbing rhythm pulsated through his body, and it felt as if his innards were in a giant washing machine. His mind control kicked in calming his bodily responses and switching to a state of cerebral serenity. He concentrated on the music and realised that he knew the tune blasting out of the walls. It was his favourite band from old-time Sheffield led by the person he was named after in the state-run kindergarten. Adi screamed at the top of his voice, "The Hacker by Clock DVA!"

Immediately everything went quiet. Adi could see the hooded figure on the screen appearing to laugh, but the eyes now seemed to be black and demonic. The picture disappeared, and in its place, an opening appeared in the wall. Adi followed his instincts and tentatively pushed his way through the opening into a long corridor lit by a shimmering blue light.

Adi slipped and slithered on the metallic floor and finally reached the end where another door opened, and he entered into a small box-like room with what looked like dentist's chair in the middle. Adi in a trance-like state sat down in the chair. Immediately restraints shot out from the chair, and before he knew what had happened, they clamped firmly around his ankles, wrists and neck.

Despair flooded through Adi, and he began mentally scolding himself for falling into such a trap. Bemused, he could not conceive who had snared him and what they wanted. Adi calmed his thoughts and blocked out his knowledge of twisted individuals and groups who would kidnap and torture citizens for their and their audience's deviant fantasies.

A screen appeared on the wall, and the familiar hooded figure from earlier came into focus with electric blue eyes staring intently at him. Adi realised that there was movement behind him despite twisting and turning he could only look straight ahead at the now flashing screen. Suddenly everything went dark, and he was aware of a figure standing in front of him raising an arm and bringing it down in a swift jabbing motion. Adi began twisting and turning in a futile effort to free himself and closed his eyes in anticipation of a blow.

Nothing happened, and Adi tentatively opened his eyes and saw a slight androgynous figure right in front of him with a small hand-held device pointing straight at him. The restraints suddenly snapped open, and he was free.

"Hello, Adi or should I call you Cyd. Pleased that you have made it so far in one piece."

Adi struggled to gather his thoughts and stared directly at the petite figure in front of him with bright red hair and diamond piercings in their eyebrows, ears and nose with wraparound black glasses obscuring their eyes.

"Pleased to meet you, at last, I am Woodward. I thought it best to meet face to face to stress the importance of your next task. As you may have realised this is the final staging post for those destined for The Farm where we extract useful information from them before their crucifixion. I thought it best that we checked that you were who you said you were and not an android imposter."

Adi shook his head and it quickly sunk in that he was going to survive, having resigned himself to meet a sticky end at the hands of some desperado terrorists. "What the chuffing Hades was all that about, Woodward if that is your name. That deafening music, this chair?"

Woodward smiled, showing brilliant white teeth sharpened to points. "The music is to differentiate between humans and androids; one of their characteristics is not being able to distinguish tunes when played at a certain decibel. Androids end up self-destructing, and it can be very messy. We needed to be certain you are who we thought you were and not a dissident infiltrator. The chair is a warning for you not to double-cross or disappoint us. The chair has physical restraints, but more interesting are the mental disturbance waves it can cause. You would beg to be pegged out on The Farm."

Adi shrugged and wondered what was going to happen next.

Woodward led Adi into another room and two technicians fussed around them both wiring them up to headsets with a large screen appearing on the wall. Adi followed Woodward into the room, marvelling at her cat-like movement. Adi was average height, about 2.8 Dra, (6ft 6ins in local parlance following the outlawing of the metric system) and towered over the diminutive Woodward.

The visuals sparked into life, and Adi winced as Woodward's voice echoed around his skull and several pictures of what seemed to be fat middle-aged men appeared on the wall-screen.

"These specimens are elite members of the ruling Politburo, and in the last six mesyats they have gone missing. We fear they have been abducted and eliminated. We need someone like yourself to seek out information about what is happening and locate the organisation behind these treasonable crimes. You will be rewarded handsomely, but the greatest incentive will be to keep your life."

Woodward chuckled and bared her pointed teeth at Adi, but the malevolence behind the message seeped through his brain and forced a shiver down his spine.

Adi concentrated on the wall-screen and absorbed the details of the missing Nomenklatura, the elite caste within the Corporation, the men who wielded all the absolute power in Steel City. These men led shadowy lives, and it was clear that although they established the rules and punishments, they did not consider that they were subject to any constraints.

Woodward, sensing the mental unease growing within Adi, broke into his thought processes and snapped at him, "You will report to me and me only, someone or some organisation is trying to de-stabilise our way of life, and we must eradicate these enemies."

Adi was concentrating hard to ensure that Woodward did not have access to all his deeper thought processes yet still managed to absorb all the information and store it in his memory banks.

The session ended, and with the implants removed from their heads, Adi was able to relax. He turned to face Woodward who flowed to her feet, smiling and purposefully exposing her dagger-like teeth as she flicked her studded tongue like a reptile about to deliver a fatal blow.

"Very near, very near" she hissed, "Nearly infiltrated your secret synapses and your heretical thoughts, Newton. Never mind, there will be a next time. Meanwhile, you have an important task to complete. Please meet your new colleagues."

CHAPTER FIVE

Woodward, with a forceful prod to Adi's back, ushered him through another opening which had suddenly appeared in the corner of the room. Adi straightened up then ducked through it and shuffled along a jet-black corridor until he emerged into a relaxation area with massage chairs, virtual reality headsets and an array of nutrition capsules and liquid refreshment jars.

Adi looked behind him, but Woodward was gone, and there was no sign of the way he had entered the room. Adi jerked around to see three figures advancing towards him, he adopted his well-honed Systema martial art defensive position and began to evaluate what was going to happen next.

Adi felt a sudden, jolting pain at the back of his neck and crumpled to the floor. He glanced up and, blinking the tears from his eyes, saw once again the cold, grinning stare of Woodward.

"Behave, Citizen Newton. They are not going to hurt you at the moment. These are the team who are going to help you solve our major problem."

The three figures all rushed to help Adi to his feet. They directed him to a massage chair and sat in a semi-circle opposite him. Adi looked around for Woodward, but she had disappeared again.

A tall, willowy woman spoke first. She had long blonde dreadlocks down to her waist and an inquisitive, pixie-like face with diamond studs in her eyebrows and a flash of a lightning tattoo on her left cheek.

"Don't get too worried about Woodward. She likes to make out she is tough, just try and avoid getting on her wrong side."

"My name is Zaf, and we are from 'Maskirovka' and my friends are Sabella and Anton."

Adi looked bewildered and asked, 'Who or what is 'Maskirovka?'"

Zaf flashed Adi a kindly smile and said, "We are the clandestine part of The Revenge and Retribution department. We are so secret, even the main Politburo of the Corporation is not aware of our existence. We are directed by Woodward."

Anton Micorevic, a huge square box of a man, spoke and in deep bass tones tinged with an Eastern Europa accent boomed, "Adi, or I think ve will call you, Cyd, ve know all about your interventions in the nethervorld. Ve are called "Maskirovka" and ve monitor all communications across the city. If necessary, ve can twist reality to confuse everybody, friends and enemies alike so that no one really knows vhat is going on. Ve aim to know everything good or bad about our citizens including you, miy druh."

Zaf continued, "We know you are a Hawking and have monitored you to ensure that you are not involved in any of the extreme dissenting disenchanted groups. We are also all Hawkings and graduated as you did with the highest marks and honours from Steel City Cybernautics. You are in a unique position in that you are highly qualified but forced to live and work outside the Hallam Village circles. We need your experience with those who operate in the cracks of society to track down the dissident group that is waging a terrorist campaign against the members of the elite *Nomenklatura*.

Zaf banged her hand on the side of her chair and said passionately, "Our lives and careers are now on the line, and we are all inextricably linked, and if you fail, we fail. As you have seen, Woodward is not a forgiving overseer and completely focused on achieving her ultimate goal."

Adi sat there looking stunned and began to regret his years of study and finishing top of his year.

Why was he a Hawking and why was he not just a nothing cog, in a factory in the arse end of Steel City, life would have been easier!

Suddenly Anton and Zaf stood up and walked towards a door which had suddenly appeared in the far corner of the room. Anton turned and said, "Udachi" and a twinkling Zaf beamed and in a sing-song accent called out, "Good luck, Cyd, dorogoy, we have our own work to complete."

Adi watched them leave and turned his gaze to the remaining member of the "Maskirovka" triumvirate who had remained silent during his conversations with Zaf and Anton. The figure stood up and beckoned Adi to follow them, "I am Sabella."

Sabella was of a similar androgynous appearance as Woodward although she had a darker tinge to her skin. She had a shaved head with a red and green snake tattooed on the right side of her face. The fangs flickered across her eyebrow with the tail disappearing down her neck into the shoulder of her tunic. Sabella had not changed her expression since Adi had first seen her and from close up, he was transfixed by her piercing purple eyes which seemed to drill deep into his soul.

Adi felt he was drifting into a dream when Sabella spoke and had to jerk himself back into reality. Sabella had a soft, voice with and unusual hypnotic quality that Adi had never encountered before.

"Cheer up Cyd, could be worse, following a cyber-personality test it has been decided that us two are the best fit to work together, like it or not."

Adi was taken aback by Sabella's friendly and welcoming tone. Her previously stern face was creased with a huge smile, and he was even more astounded to see the fangs of the snake still flicker as if they were ready to strike.

Sabella said with a chortle, "Snap out of it, boy, we've work to do. You've seen the pictures of the missing citizens. Now we need to look at what we know, alright."

They were escorted out of the room by a couple of robot sentries and taken to a transportation room. There they were kitted out with transponders which would scramble their cells, speed them through the cyber ether and reassemble them on arrival allowing them to rematerialize seconds after they set off. Adi had heard of this means of travelling within the confines of the metropolis, but had not himself had the privilege of experiencing it. Adi had no time to worry about what was going to happen when everything went blank, and he found himself back in his office at the Western Works. An amused looking Sabella with her alluring snake tattoo was already sitting at his desk and studying his cyber screen.

"You took your time boy, where you been? We nearly lost you out there. You could have ended up spread over the whole of Steel City. I think in the future you had better keep to normal modes of transportation. Just been adding some information on our missing citizens to your memory chip, alright."

Sabella stood up and winked making her snake's fangs flicker and with a friendly grin said, "See you tomorrow at chasov, (10.30 am)," and at that Sabella disappeared with the words, "Make sure you have caught up with info I've left, alright boy..." hanging in the air.

Adi slumped in his chair and put his throbbing head in his hands and realised how much he was sweating. His thoughts were racing, and he began assessing and reassessing how he might get himself out of this mess. Most of his life Adi had been able to blag his way out of dangerous situations, but reality struck, and he realised that this time there was no way out.

Adi woke up, aching all over and stretching his neck still painful from Woodward's blow and from sleeping at his cyber desk. He had slept fitfully and remembered dreaming about a giant, smiling snake sinking its fangs into his scarred cheek.

Adi shuddered and clicked his favourite Clock DVA track on to play filling the room with discordant chords and wailing saxophones underpinned by an electric drum beat. 'High Holy Disco Mass' immediately lightened his mood and further improved by chewing on an old-fashioned mood enhancer tablet purchased from an illicit supplier based in the Hospital at Attercliffe.

CHAPTER SIX

The tall, patrician figure of Count Salman Mubarak strode purposefully through the 'Merch-Centre' at the Western Works. He expected the throngs of ordinary people to get out of his way as they darted from emporium to emporium to try and purchase vitals to keep them and their families alive.

The Count spotted the Virtual Reality Pleasure Palace he was looking for and ignored the black visored security personnel and entered the receptacle area and took the anti-gravity beam to the VIP area. He found the door with the name of his intended assignation, Violetta Valery and keyed in the code he had been provided with by secure cyber-mail. The Count entered through the security lock and came face to face with Violetta but did not see the two dark-suited figures appear behind him and hit him with the force of a lightning bolt.

CHAPTER SEVEN

Adi slipped out of his office pod and caught the Tuk Tram to Leadmill, the central transport hub. The area was overrun with small, independently run Coffshops to take advantage of all the travellers and commuters. Each Coffshop had small individual booths where you could meet in private to ensure no one was eavesdropping physically or remotely. Adi backtracked and double-tracked for shest (30 mins) to ensure that no one was following him. Eventually, he entered one called Black Mamba that Sabella had identified for their liaison that morning.

He did not realise he was under surveillance from a miniature drone. This drone had the appearance of one of the many bluebottle flies that plagued the outside areas attracted by feeding opportunities at The Farm.

Adi ruminated over the new information that had been given to him and wondered what had he not been told. As far as he knew at least five high ranking officials from the higher echelons of the elite politburo had gone missing. Their personal microchips indicated their life force had expired, but the directional

25

information had been blocked. It appeared they had all been visiting addresses in areas well out of the elite residential and work complexes before their disappearance.

The officials named were Ivan Starikov, Ashton Lukashenko, Count Salman Mubarak with two others remaining anonymous. Adi assumed they must be higher-ranking officials, and news of their disappearance could cause major embarrassment if it got out. The reasons for the visits had not been made clear, but from Adi's experience, they were not likely to have been on official business and probably seeking hedonistic gratification.

Adi knew that all elite members had access to all the latest virtual reality entertainment hubs as well as being able to tap into individual androids for personal attention. However, many of the privileged had become bored and disillusioned with what was on offer and would seek out illicit human contact and illegally produced narcotics and sugar drinks.

Adi had made mental notes on his cyber bracelet which was part of his personal commtel system. He had highlighted areas he needed to seek further information from Sabella and ideas on they were going to start cracking this case.

Sabella was already in the interactive meeting place and had just finished checking the area for surveillance devices. She had not found anything and smiled when Adi ducked through the titanium aperture. Two drinks appeared through the table and Adi was taken aback to see it was his favourite honey lassi concoction. Sabella saw the look of surprise on Adi's face and chuckled as she said, "Cyd, Cyd, my boy, I know more about you than you do!"

"You have been given the permitted details regarding the missing elite members but happy to put some decaying flesh on their bones, so to speak." Sabella grinned at Adi.

"They appear to have been involved in a sort of 'Hell Fire and Damnation Club'" possibly inspired by the revival of a few years ago of a fascination with Aleister Crowley and Necromancy. All were members of the Nomenklatura, and there have been rumours of widespread abuse across vulnerable members of society."

Adi interjected, "Never, thought that had died out after the show trials a decade ago, and everyone involved was zeroed."

Sabella laughed out aloud with a strange, staccato, metallic sound, "Cyd, for a supposed man of experience you have a lot to learn, boy. Yes, numbers outside the elite were eliminated, but the ones on the Corporation side of the security wall were merely admonished and monitored for a short period. In hindsight, probably not the most sensible option and I am sure someone has paid for that leniency. What happens when the elite judge themselves, boy!"

Adi began to feel irritated at being called "boy" by this woman years younger than him and the implication that he knew nothing about the machinations of the ruling classes.

Sabella seemed to take pleasure at his annoyance but then said "We need to get serious. This is what they were up to, the pleasure domes with their reality games, sports, cyber fantasies were not enough for them. They succumbed to a desire for human flesh. They were not content with the best that our cyber entertainers had to offer but wanted the officially forbidden carnal pleasure with humans of all three sexes rather than the permitted androids."

Adi looked perplexed and eventually spoke, "So, they were visiting the loppy regions of the city. I'm surprised they were not spotted and exposed."

"Here's the rub, dear Cyd, as far as we can see they visited dwelling pods all over the City, but when we tracked them down, the pods were empty, swept physically and electronically clean. The only sign that anyone has been there is an anatomical part often left in a specimen jar that we have linked by DNA to our missing persons."

Adi spluttered, "Ey up, is that right, they all have been mutilated and murdered then?"

Sabella smirked, "The removal of this certain part of their anatomy does not necessarily mean they are dead, but life would be very different for them! All information we have tells us they have paid with their lives for their unnatural desires."

Sabella carried on with a more serious tone, "We have cracked cyber codes for messages that have arranged trysts with several individuals. We have unearthed a profusion of names including, "Violette Valery", "Sonya Marmeladova", "Valerie Tasso", "Lulu White", "Veronica Franco" and "Su Xiao Xiao". It is not clear if they are separate people, but we now think they are all linked. It does appear that there is a sophisticated cybersecurity organisation backing them because even our top technicians are struggling to get any further information. It is almost as if they are fully knowledgeable about our processes and security systems."

Adi stretched and realised he needed to pee, despite all the innovations and technological advances; when you have to go, you have to go. Adi made his excuses to Sabella who agreed to order some more drinks.

CHAPTER EIGHT

Adi left the meeting area and followed the glowing lights pointing the way to the restroom area. Adi was preoccupied with his thoughts about what he had managed to get himself involved with and a nagging sense of impending doom. He barely noticed two masked figures enter the room and was just buttoning his jump-suit when one of them hit in the kidney area with a steel baton. The other assailant hit him across the back of his legs, dropping him to the floor.

A heavy boot crunched on the back of his head and pinned to the ground with the metal rod. Adi managed to splutter, "What the chuffing hell, geroff, what you doing? Take all my credits if you want..."

The first figure jabbed him in the spine, which took his breath away and suddenly one of them spoke with a harsh, metallic voice seemingly doctored by a device to hide their real voice.

"Back off, you are messing with the wrong people, next time we will be serious, this is a warning."

Adi grimaced as he was struck again, this time across his buttocks but felt a sense of relief as he sensed his assailants leaving the room. He staggered to his feet, stretching his arms above his head, already feeling the aches and pains from his beating. Adi rushed to the door and ran along the corridor leading to the exit to try and spot his assailants.

Adi was panting heavily, and his heart was racing as he turned the corner into the main atrium. In front of him was Sabella with two prone bodies on the floor. They did not look like the thugs he had briefly glimpsed. Sabella was in communication with someone on her wrist-comm.

Sabella looked surprised to see him, and with no hint of a smile and steel in her eyes, she produced a laser pen from inside her tunic and quickly pointed it at the heads of the unconscious miscreants in turn and shot a beam of light through their skulls. At the same time, a detachment of elite security enforcement officers poured into the room. Half of them scooped up the bodies from the floor and hurriedly left. The rest bundled Sabella and Adi back into their meeting booth. They checked that Sabella was ok and immediately left to catch up with their colleagues.

Adi sat down and with the adrenalin dissipating began to feel his injuries. "What the hell happened? Feel like gipping, bastards. Why did you finish those two thugs off, surely we could have found out who they were and where they were from?" Adi stopped himself from protesting further; his suspicions about Sabella and the whole fucking set up began to drown out his rational thoughts.

Sabella smiled again, and her eyes sparkled as she handed Adi some blister tablets. "Here you are Cyd, my boy, have some Valerian shots, these will take the pain away and stop you pissing blood for days. Your assailants managed to give us the slip, but its best to say that they were caught when we report back to Woodward. The patsies were a couple of low life criminals my security forces found lurking in the vicinity trying to deal illicit drugs. No one will miss them, boy!"

Adi exasperated said, "How did you know they went for my kidneys? Sure you don't know anything about those two bastards who did this?"

Sabella laughed and said, "Look my neck is as much on the line here as yours, cool it. We need to agree on what we do next to track down this organisation behind all this mayhem and our important missing dignitaries. I watched it all by drone and would have intervened if they had done more than trying to warn you off."

33

CHAPTER NINE

Adi walked along the dark corridor that led to the Paradise complex of dwelling pods and communal dormitories that housed the migrant workforce and those individuals who wanted to live off the grid. All areas of the metropolis were connected by hastily built tunnels to alleviate the dangers of having to move around the city where the outside temperature soared to a level that was dangerous and toxic.

The authorities largely ignored Paradise. The place was ruled by draconian self-appointed militia gangs who oversaw all the illegal activity. Adi had been ordered, as part of Woodward and Sabella's plan, to track down the organisation responsible for the kidnapping of the elite committee members to move into Paradise as a resident.

Sabella explained that the IT gurus had tracked some electronic messages to areas inside Paradise. If the organisation they were seeking was not based in Paradise, it was using facilities there to coordinate its actions. Adi was moving there in the guise of a recently released criminal who had spent years in the local gulag at Attercliffe. Sabella had ordered him to immerse himself in the lawless society to try and get a lead on the cyber terrorists who were picking off members of the ruling elite.

Adi had travelled to Paradise on the creaking Tuk Transit system which followed the old tram lines in the metropolis with cheaply constructed tunnels and shelters to protect from the burning sun. In the tunnels and the covered pathways to the areas where people lived were many commercial enterprises, *Bagnios, Serails, Sugar Cafes* and the latest fad, *Jelly Houses*. These were the reason why many inhabitants were able to cope with the horrendous living and working conditions seeking solace in illicit food, drink, drugs, and temptations of the flesh.

Adi liked walking around the metropolis and knew his way better than most inhabitants and in particular the security forces. He also had links to many of the diverse community groups and criminal organisations through his work. Adi took a mental note of all the social spaces as he followed the directions to his new living environment. Adi was also acutely aware that he was being watched as he progressed through the covered pathways from the Tuk tram halt, knowing full well that the local criminals would be taking note of anyone new in the area.

Adi crossed a square by a particularly lively Jelly House and preferring to take a straight line to his destination he turned into a narrow *jennel*. His senses began to twitch as he strode down the tight passageway, suddenly two figures appeared in front of him and as he glanced behind him realised that there were at least two more following him.

Adi adopted his well-practised defensive stance and began to quickly assess who his potential assailants were. Adi realised that these four were not an organised criminal gang but young blades out for a bit of sport, rolling punters from the nearby Jelly House. Many of these punters would be worse for wear and would accept losing a few credits to these young thugs if they held back on the kicks and thumps.

The first blade lunged at Adi with a steel baton but was surprised when Adi deftly grabbed his wrist, and his face crunched against Adi's knee. He fell to the ground groaning and clutching his broken nose with blood spurting through his fingers.

Two of the remaining blades realising that they were not dealing with the usual spaced out punter approached Adi from different sides. Adi using his martial art skills began striking out with legs and fists frantically blocking their attacks. Adi's superior strength and skills eventually allowed him to subdue his two opponents, one paralysed by a blow to the spine and the other hampered by a shattered knee cap.

Adi stretched his arms out and clicked his back, recovering from the effort of battling the assailants when he remembered there had been four of them—hoping that the final blade had scarpered to save their own skin. As Adi turned, he realised that he had miscalculated and a steel baton struck him on the shoulder, and a kick from a heavy-duty boot hit him in the stomach causing him to collapse to the hard ground gasping for air.

The blade was grinning as he stood over his armed flexed as he prepared to bring his weapon down on his victim's head. Adi winced and tried to protect his head, allowing the blade to connect with his ribs with a short, jabbing kick.

The blade spat at Adi and shouted, "You malchick bastard, this is for my fellow blades." With arm drawn back, his whole body lit up with a ghostly halo of sparky light, and his body began to shake uncontrollably. Adi looked up, smelling burning as the lifeless thug twitched from the massive jolt of electricity that had destroyed his life force.

Two figures appeared, it was Zaf and Anton Micorevic, from the Maskirovka. Anton just glowered at Adi as he stowed his laser gun back inside his jacket.

Adi dragged himself up from the floor tenderly rubbing his shoulder and damaged ribs. Zaf smiled and said, "It was a good job that Woodward wanted us to make sure you arrived at your destination in one piece. Quick, we must leave before the local militia arrives to investigate what has happened to these vermin."

They quickly ushered Adi away from the Bagnio and entered a nearby Sugar Café, Adi and Zaf sat down, and Anton collected some sugar shots from the counter. Zaf offered him some pills to counteract the pain from his injuries. Adi shrugged thinking that this was becoming a habit.

Adi greedily swallowed the pills followed by a double sugar shot and spreading his hands wide looked at his rescuers and plaintively asked, "Ever since I became involved with Woodward and your crew, I have had massive grief, and I am lucky to be in one piece. Who knows what is going on and who is out to get me?"

Zaf interrupted and said, "Just bad chance, no one outside our circle knows what is happening and what you are supposed to be doing. We must be off, work to do, stay safe."

Adi looked suspiciously across the table at Zaf and Anton as they finished their shots, quickly stood up, and totally ignoring Adi they jogged out of the door with Anton talking on his wrist-comm device.

CHAPTER TEN

Adi closed the electronic door behind him and looked around at his new home, a large communications screen dominated the room with artificial light emanating from all corners of the square room. He pushed buttons on a rectangular pad on the glass table in the far corner and checked out the sleeping area which emerged from the wall as did the bathroom and kitchen area.

Adi plugged his personal computer chip into the device at the back of the glass table and started checking through all the information he had been given and started to formulate his plan of action. His device pinged as new messages began to arrive with more background information on the missing elite individuals. One of the messages was marked urgent; it gave details of a new person who had gone missing overnight.

Adi began to contemplate what the hell he had let himself in for, particularly that he had been physically attacked numerous times and was seemingly under surveillance from unknown sources. Adi had courted danger in his detective work but usually knew the parameters and who to avoid and how to stay in one piece.

Life had seemed much simpler when he was graduating from university and appeared destined for a role as a cog in the mechanics of the establishment. He wondered if he had not been such a rebel, he might have had a more straight- forward existence.

The group of dissidents behind these attacks on members of the elite must be well equipped and trained to have escaped the scrutiny of the secret services. They must have someone who had undergone a similar level of training in the 'dark arts' as he had. Adi brought up class lists for the last five years and tried to identify any students who had gone rogue like himself. The majority he found had taken the safe option of working for the establishment. Adi narrowed the lists down further by eliminating those executed for treason and those who had undergone complete mental breakdowns. Eventually, he was left with a list of those who had simply disappeared, but sensed some names were missing.

Adi now had a list of three possible suspects that he would pursue via his cyber investigations to see if they may have had reasons for attacking members of the ruling establishment. Adi hacked into the official network and began trying to identify illegal activity with other people nearby who were surfing on the dark side. Adi identified a link in the surrounding buildings, but every time he tried to pinpoint the signal he was blocked. In what was a cat and mouse game Adi tried all his expertise to outwit his cyber opponent and get a bearing on their whereabouts.

Adi realised that this had to be someone of high expertise who had probably received expert training in cyber espionage. They may be working for a high-level criminal organisation as part of a team of experts. Suddenly Adi latched on to a chink in their electronic defence and for microseconds obtained a screengrab of an area in the flat complex next door to where he was. Within a flash, the link was blocked. Adi was able to break the connection, having obtained the information he required, Adi quickly brought up a map of the immediate area and narrowed his quarry down to three pods in the top corner of the building. The location of the pods was outlined in red, identifying them as restricted areas of the accommodation unit.

Adi decided to take a walk around the local area and see how difficult it would be to get into the restricted pods and clarify why they were categorised as access denied for ordinary citizens. Adi was perplexed, and it soon dawned on him that this was not an official blocking but had perhaps been set up by the criminal gang to protect their operational base.

Adi used his electronic lock picking skills learnt from one of the most highly skilled and notorious cyber thieves that he had helped catch, they had done a deal, and Adi had acquired his skills and professional expertise. The court commuted the criminal's death sentence, and instead, he was committed to a long stretch in the Attercliffe gulag. Within three years, Cedric the Cat had completely lost his marbles. After this, he was found to be mentally ill and as a result sent to die in The Killing Field exposed to the burning heat.

Adi forced his way into the service hatch for the area of the building where the three protected pods were. He then extracted the passcodes for each of the three dwelling spaces from the secure control panel.

Adi made his way into the first pod bypassing the alarm guard and the CCTV. He ducked into the pod and very quickly realised that it was empty. There was no sign of life and no evidence of any electronic equipment.

Adi left the pod and gained entrance to the adjoining pod in a similar manner. On entering, he found the same situation as the previous dwelling with no obvious sign of life or that anyone had been there in recent times. Again, there was no electronic equipment or even a screen on the wall.

Adi steeled himself for the third pod, wondering if this was all an electronic cyber smokescreen and he was in the wrong place.

Adi tiptoed into the last dwelling place and was immediately blinded by a bright flash and deafened by a piercing noise. Everything suddenly went quiet, and Adi realised he could not move his legs; in fact, he was unable to move anything. He tried to reach his protective weapon in the inside pocket of his tunic, but his arm did not respond to his frantic mental messages.

CHAPTER ELEVEN

Adi's eyes were still functioning, and with his peripheral vision, he sensed something moving towards him. Yet again, he began to fear the worst and that no one would really care that he was gone.

There was a strange hissing sound, and a floating chair appeared in front of him. These were the equivalent of old-fashioned wheelchairs for people unable to walk. Only people from the elite classes used them as anyone who was or became disabled in the lower orders were rewarded with a quick one-way trip to The Killing Field.

The hoverchair floated on a cushion of air; controlled via a headset worn by the person in it. The chair turned to face him, and he realised that it was flanked by two androids who despite their non-human qualities, looked keen to rip him to bits like rabid metallic Rottweilers.

The person in the chair came into focus, and he realised that he was looking at what appeared to be a young child. Adi frantically searched his memory banks to recollect where he had seen that face before.

45

"Hello, again, Adi Newton, surely you remember me, a fellow Hawking scholar. I was in the intake below you, but we nonetheless collaborated for a period on the Venusian Project. Good to see you again. Sorry, I will release you from your electronic cage, a little invention of mine. Don't worry these two won't bite, unless I tell them to, haha! Meet Sioux and Patti my carers and protectors, haha!"

"Haha Harry, wasn't it?" Adi slowly recalled, "You were top of everything, but no one really knew why you were there, unlike all the other "differently abled" chuffs who were never allowed into Hawking College, is that right?"

"Forget the Ha Ha bit, Newton, you are not in a position to take the piss now, unless you want an intimate chat with my two friends here, relax, I think we can mutually help each other, I know what mission you have been sent on... Haha!"

"Ok, Harry it is then, can I sit down, I'll take a listen, and you can tell us all this is all about?".

Adi stretched his arms out and dropped down on to a low bench and Harry manoeuvred his hoverchair down so that he was alongside him at the same eye level. A large screen emerged from the wall, and Adi recognised his newly allocated pod. A number of figures were searching the area.

Harry struck up saying, "See, you are much better off here, I don't think you realise who is on your side and who is working against you. Well, we can work together to our mutual benefit or I can let you be eaten alive or worse caught by goons like those on the screen, Ha Ha!"

Adi began to speak, "But what the f...". Harry interrupted Adi, and looking him in the eye and in a condescending tone said, "You need a bit of catch up, me pal, sit back and watch this little vid I put together; hopefully, it will restore some of your memory banks wiped when they let you go from that bastard Hawking College, Haha!"

The drop-down screen burst into life with a group playing some music. Adi realised it was from The Stunt Kites another band from the same era as his favourites, Clock DVA, playing "Beautiful People" which then mixed into "Genetic Warfare" by Vice Versa.

Harry said over the music, "I know you are a massive fan of Clock DVA, but even you must realise that there were other combos worth listening to, Haha!" Harry continued, "Thought would bring some light relief to a serious subject and yes I know Vice Versa transformed into those poppy wanksters ABC, Haha!"

Adi watched the unfolding tale on the screen with horror as the events earlier in the century unfolded. Adi felt a nagging pain in his synapses. Some of the events on screen seemed familiar, but even with his best effort, he could not locate the memories anywhere. It was as if they had been blanked out.

Harry with a concerned tone said, "Yes, it will be difficult, these memories were torn out of your brain electronically as you were cast adrift from Hawking College and being a member of the so-called ruling elite, ha Fucking ha!!"

Adi watched in rapt fascination the history lesson laid before him. The destruction of much of mainland Europa showing in vivid technicolour as The Europan army played high stakes poker with the newly reformed Sovok Socialist Republic. What had been Germany, Holland and France was flattened before retaliatory strikes could be made. However, the resulting radioactive fallout decimated much of the lands that were Ukrainye. The two major enemy countries had laid fallow the majority of the territory they were fighting over.

The next section was about the de-globalization of the world, continents, countries and even partitions of nations. Subsequent viruses had swept across the globe and only kept under control with the cessation of trave, tourism and all trade and commerce expected to take place electronically. Online games of all description grew as spectator sports were shunned and eventually outlawed. These conditions coincided with the growth of militant climate change groups who were keen to curtail most air flights and any transport fuelled by non-renewable energy. For a while, this improved the state of the world. Still, the cataclysmic weather conditions of 2043 put an end to this as temperatures across the globe increased by 10%, making many areas inhospitable and even areas formerly in Angleterre extremely hot. The population had to stay indoors to survive. Adi felt like he was being fed chunks of information that began to allow the jigsaw to start making sense.

Angleterre, as it was, had been divided into historic ceremonial politburos based on the large conurbations with the majority of the surviving population living in purpose-built housing units such as Paradise in Steel City. Adi realised that this was not totally unfamiliar to him and that although this was the way of life for the majority of the existing populace, there was another elite level of society.

Harry spoke sharply breaking Adi's concentration, "Yes, the next bit is about those parasites of society who don't have to live in sweltering, rat and cat infested sheds like most of us. Many of our fellow students from Hawking College have very different existences than us. Haha!"

Adi piped up, "Aye, I know about Hallam Village where the elite live, in better conditions than the rest of us, if only we had toed the line eh, Harry?"

"Haha!" chortled Harry, his round face creased up like a punch ball, his eyes sparkling like purple stars in the heavens." You only know the half of it, my friend. The real elite, The Sovoks live beyond Hallam in the Dore Resort. They revel in complete luxury and are free to travel and consort with whomever they want. They live off the credits earned from exploiting the workforce in areas like Paradise and the factory units all around Steel City. It is some these parasites who are being eliminated, and the ones you have been sent to investigate, haha!"

"Hang on a chuffing microsec, Ha Ha Harry Haslam, how do you know this?" Adi asked angrily, sweat forming on his brow and trickling down his spine, "Is it you and your paranoid androids that I am trying to track down?" Adi continued getting increasingly breathless as he looked around for a means of escape but realised that the two robots were guarding the only exit from the pod.

"This were supposed to be a top-secret mission given to me by high-level security bods. How the fuck does tha know what's going on? Looks like you have skewered me before I have properly started" Adi continued while the smile on Harry's balloon-like face grew wider and wider as Adi appeared to be sinking deeper into a panicked funk.

CHAPTER TWELVE

Vladimir Stankovich let himself out of his apartment block in Dore Resort and strolled along the ice-cold, air-conditioned corridor to catch transport to the entertainment/leisure complex at Western Works. Vladimir had just arrived from an international trip to Ottoman Central to finalise a financial deal with another ruling oligarch and was very pleased with himself. He had decided that he needed some downtime and was looking forward to some hedonistic pleasure. He had already taken some Quak pills to enhance his sexual performance. Vladimir was massively overweight and was way above the strict guidelines that the ordinary masses were supposed to adhere to and severely punished if they did not.

Vladimir waddled along to the lift area and suddenly stopped in his tracks as two figures appeared on both sides of him. They were wearing black hoods with a narrow slit which showed their glowing red eyes. Vladimir began shouting for them to get away as he was an important member of the elite politburo. The noise suddenly stopped as the figure on his right held a glowing handheld device to Vladimir's blubbery neck.

He shook and collapsed towards the floor. Before he struck the ground, the two figures effortlessly lifted him between them and walked quickly to the emergency exit by the corner of the lifts.

CHAPTER THIRTEEN

Harry hovered towards Adi, and the grin disappeared from his round face. He clicked his fingers, and his two robots appeared behind him.

Adi braced himself and waited to see what was going to happen; he realised there was no way out and was resigned to his fate.

"Haha ha ha!" giggled Harry, "looks like I had you fooled Newton, you always were a trifle gullible, chill out man, we are on the same side."

The robotic pair disappeared to one of the other rooms, and Harry manoeuvred himself alongside Adi pointing to the wall where the began screen glow.

Adi still felt confused about what was going on when the giant monitor on the wall flickered to life once more. Gradually a figure appeared and the focus distilled to a glaring, brutally angular face which began to speak showing pointed teeth set in unsmiling lips. Adi realised that it was Woodward who had promised dire recriminations if he did not make any progress in his task.

Woodward's spiked teeth shone as she began to speak. "It is good, Citizen Newton that you have made contact with Harry Haslam, treat him with the utmost respect as he is my kin. Everything will be explained as to the next stage of your task."

Adi glanced at Harry whose round face was bright red with sweat forming on his domed forehead. Harry gave an embarrassed look and said, "Every time without fail my mother manages to show me up...... Haha!"

"Be quiet Harold, I need to give you both an update before you take the next steps. You thought you could hide away from me, Harold, but it did not take Citizen Newton long to track you down. I am glad to see you are looking well but now is the time for you to cease your frivolous ways and work for the good of Steel City and our cause."

Adi looked like he had been dealt "The Dead Man's Hand" in an online million credit game of poker. He was supposed to be in the top percentage intelligence wise of the population, but at the moment he felt like the lowest skin scraper on The Killing Field.

Woodward boomed, "For Stalin's sake, it comes to something when I have to rely on such gormless specimens as you two! Listen up another elite member disappeared last night. That useless and corpulent member of the Nomenklatura, Vladimir Stankovich was attacked and disappeared last night. But this time it was from an elite area, not the stinking rat holes that the others were visiting for their bodily gratification."

Harry interrupted Woodward, "But this means that whoever is undertaking this campaign have access to the......"

Woodward now shouting, "Be quiet, Harold, of course, I know what this means, and I will be sending you both instructions by vidtech so listen and act, you dullards."

The monitor flickered, and Woodward began to fade from the screen. Harry and Adi shared a knowing glance, and both let out a collective sigh. The screen flickered back into life, it was Woodward again, "Don't trust anyone, I need you both to get through this in one piece, stay safe."

The display abruptly blanked. Sioux and Patti immediately appeared in front of Harry and Adi and offered them drinks in shiny gold goblets.

Adi accepted the drink and clinked cups with Harry; it was zoom juice, full of vitamins, ginseng and a shot of psychobin guaranteed to cheer the spirits and improve concentration and decision making. Zoom was usually very difficult to get hold of outside the elite areas of Steel City. Still, Harry had a stash, and they both knocked it back, giving the empty receptacles back to the brooding robots who returned to the galley area.

Adi said "Thanks pal" in the direction of Harry, "But, look, you need to level with me, what the chuffing fuck is going on and what's with this mother business with that ice queen Woodward? You must be kidding me that she is your birth matryoshka, or maybe that makes sense eh, Ha Ha Harry. No wonder you didn't end up at The Killing Field and how you managed to be taken on at Hawking College, friends in high places eh, Ha Ha?"

Harry looked shamefaced but suddenly perked up, a broad grin lighting up his circular features. "So, don't fuck with me Newton, Woodward is not to be messed with, and even though there is not a great deal of affection between us there is that lineage loyalty between us, unlike all you others who haven't a clue who begat you, haha!"

Harry then clicked a switch on the black belt across his chest, "All right Newton, I have disconnected the vidicomm block on this area for your communication device. I suggest you use the next desyat (10) minut to check your messages to see what Woodward has arranged for you, Ha Ha!"

Adi felt a continuous pulse from his wristband indicating there were a string of missed calls and messages backing up on his wristcomm device. Adi scrawled down the list and realised that the majority of messages were from Sabella who, with each communication she left, was getting increasingly agitated. Adi returned the last call, and Sabella's stern face appeared on the screen, "Cyd, my boy where have you been? I thought you had done a runner or been carved up by one of those roaming gangs of blades in that cesspit you call Paradise. Get your lazy arse to Leadmill prompt tomorrow, or I will arrange for you to be done to a crisp, ok boy."

Adi's hackles rose as Sabella's aggressive tone irritated him. The parting words from Woodward also put him on edge, and he mumbled assent.

Sabella almost spat out her orders, "Sem utra (7am) on the dot at Leadmill transport hub, you will be met by Zaf and Anton, make sure you are not followed and be alone. Woodward is not pleased with the lack of progress, and you would not want her on your case, boy!"

Everything went blank as Sabella cut the link, Adi scanned the rest of the messages and could see nothing urgent except one missed missive from Ched Parris, a small-time gangster who often fed him information in return for credits and illicit pharmaceuticals. Adi went to return the call when Harry appeared hovering in front of him and with a flourish, switched his communication blocker back on. Adi's communication device went blank, and Harry laughed, "Ha blackout ha! You will have to use it when you leave in the morning; I cannot afford to leave communication lines open for long, wouldn't want anyone undesirable tracking me down, haha!"

CHAPTER FOURTEEN

Adi had slept fitfully with strange dreams weaving in out of the characters he had recently met with everyone having snake-like faces with sharpened fangs and dagger-like slithering tongues. Adi jumped awake with a start and realised he was dripping with sweat and his heart was thumping like a beating drum. Adi grabbed his personal music device and fumbled to play some tunes to try and calm himself down.

"Knife Slits Water" by A Certain Ratio cranked up to a high volume crashed loudly around his sleeping pod, and Adi began to get his emotions under control as he chilled to the familiar beat of some sounds from a long time ago. The track ended, and Adi was now back in charge and ready to get himself sorted for his trip to Leadmill. Adi would also have to say farewell to Harry who he now felt quite attached to and hoped he was one of the few people he could trust.

Adi dressed and went into the main living area of the pod and was confronted there by Harry hovering in front of the screen flanked by his two robot protectors, Sioux and Patti.

Harry said quietly, "What the hell was going on last night, you were shouting and screaming, thought someone had managed to get in here and was slaughtering you. Good job that Sioux was on the ball and checked you were ok before starting firing indiscriminately. You ok? Haha!"

Adi rubbed his face with his hands and quietly responded, "Since all this started, I have been getting worse and worse mardy nightmares, almost as if old memories are awakening in various corners of my brain. Not chuffing helped by your film show. Hopefully, one day it will make some sense. Buried dreams slowly coming to the surface, not good Harry but thanks for asking ok, pal."

Harry, for once looking serious, a frown splitting his circular face, clicked his fingers and the large monitor came on. "Look at this" he pointed with a stubby thumb to the action unfolding on the screen, "Complete lockdown, Newton my friend, the militia have sealed off Paradise and are searching for and arresting malcontents. Not sure of the reason but authorities are keen to let everyone know what they are doing. Been several laser fights already and it is clear there have been casualties. They are hauling others off to The Killing Field. It looks as if you are going to struggle to get to Leadmill as instructed, haha!"

Adi watched the screen avidly as another group of the black-clad militia goons smashed their way into a Sugar Bar and began laying into the cowering patrons.

"Need to get to Leadmill by sem utra or will have the Maskirovka after my blood, may have to call in a few favours eh Harry, let me speak to Ched who messaged me last night."

"Ok", said Harry, "But you will need to make arrangements for two as Woodward has ordered me to send one of my robotic protectors with you, who do you want Sioux or Patti?"

Adi punched in the code and waited for Ched Parris to answer. After a few seconds, there was an answer, and Ched started talking immediately, "Cyd, have some interesting info for you about that last chat we had, just need your promise of a little award."

Adi interrupted, "Forget that for a moment Ched, have somert else for you to sort out that will pay reyt better. You need to get me and a friend to Leadmill by sem utra."

Ched laughed loudly, "You are off your balance mate, what with all those militia thugs doing everyone over, stopping innocent people earning a credit."

Adi interjected, "I know how you get around Ched, pal, get me on one of your details picking up poor souls for The Killing Field and you can drop us off at Leadmill."

"How the Hades did you know about that? Will cost you mate, big time."

Adi nodded his head at the screen, "Whatever you want, Ched, snap or spice, it's yours if tha can pull this off."

Ched hung up and messaged Adi where he needed to be in within the next tridtsat minut.

Adi showed the location to Harry who said, "That's not far away, Sioux will guide you. Better get ready, haha!"

"Why have you chosen Sioux to accompany me not Patti, Ha Ha Harry?"

Harry chortled and said, "You will find that Sioux is programmed to protect you, but I have overridden her "shall not kill" command and can be as ruthless as any psych killer, ha brutal ha!"

CHAPTER FIFTEEN

Adi and his new companion, the android Sioux left through the secret hatch in the kitchen area of the pod. They ended up in a dark service corridor lit by dull lights and the only noise the humming of the groaning air conditioning system trying to keep the crumbling building at an acceptable temperature. Sioux took the lead, and at a brisk pace, the duo hurried along the twisting corridors until they reached a security door leading to one of the communal areas of the Paradise entertainment complex.

Sioux had been given the directions for the meet with Ched Parris, and she put a steel arm across Adi's chest to prevent him from moving any further. Adi began to ponder how he would communicate with this hunk of electronic circuits with a lethal menace that Harry had loaned him.

Suddenly a sharp pain shot across his skull and a metallic voice echoed around his brain. "Careful what you are thinking Newton, my master. Harry has set up an electronic link between you and me so we can communicate without anyone else having any idea what is happening. Other people will just consider me a drone robot worker programmed to complete assigned tasks." Adi looked amazed as the metallic high pitched feminine voice that echoed in his skull transformed into an almost seductive tone that seemed to calm and soothe his anxieties. "And, less of the electronic junk comments, ok, dear."

Adi smiled as he followed Sioux out into the massive hanger like area, thinking, "if the authorities don't finish me off, I now need to cope with a lovesick robot, Satan help me!" Adi made sure he blocked his thoughts as strongly as he could and avoided looking at Sioux as she marched towards the rendezvous point.

Everything was quiet with the lockdown in force, and luckily there were no signs of any goon squads. The duo arrived outside the main Medical Stores building, usually a bustling and thriving area with people hustling and bidding for medication and lifesaving drugs.

Suddenly a group of figures appeared from a side door. Three humans clad in full-length white jumpsuits with matching balaclavas all printed with the official Steel City logo on and three robots looking very odd in official Steel City peaked caps. Ched greeted them, "For fuck's sake Cyd, quick, get in that door and get an outfit on," he also threw a cap at Sioux who looked like she was squaring up to him. Sioux caught the cap and daintily placed it on her robotic head.

Adi scuttled through the door and after a short time he reappeared, his overalls blending in with the other workers and was immediately joined by Sioux who stood almost too close at his shoulder.

The whole group stood to attention as a jogging group of the black-clad militia appeared from around the corner and pointed their laser weapons at them. One, taller than the rest, presumably the leader stepped forward, a red stripe on his arm signifying his importance. Ched quickly thrust himself forward and passed him an electronic device.

The leader of the goons peered at the screen and shouted, "Chityre rabochiye and chityre robot, check, get on with it, where are you heading?"

"Leadmill, lider, yes we are straight off now, tak lider."

The militia squad stamped their feet in unison and moved off in a synchronised march towards the main living areas of the Paradise complex.

Ched sighed heavily, "Jumped up droogs, give a human a uniform and a laser pistol and they become bullies of very little brain, come on group, let's get weaving, Leadmill here we come." Ched turned and looked at Adi and his shadow Sioux, "We need to get you safely to your destination without any further distractions, buck up, let's go!"

Ched led the group towards the Tuk transit station, where they all assembled on the empty platform and before too long a decrepit tram ground to a halt. They clambered on board, for once they had the pick of the seats due to the lockdown. The lone conductor ignored them as they were all clad in their official Steel City outfits. The tram trundled on, still stopping at all the halts even though no one left or boarded.

CHAPTER SIXTEEN

At The Cossack, the penultimate one before Leadmill, four figures boarded at the far end, it was difficult to tell if they were security: fellow Steel City workers or renegades ignoring the lockdown. Adi as always was vigilant about his surroundings and clocked that they appeared to be on Comtel devices and one if not two of them were taking a close interest in the Steel City workers.

The tram lurched to a halt, and Ched led his team out onto the platform. From here, they made their way to the escalator, which would take them to the surface and the exit. Adi was at the back of the group and realised that just before the tram left the four figures jumped from the closing doors and gathered themselves together with one still on their Comtel device. They began to stride purposefully towards the group ignoring the exit sign to their immediate right. Adi sensed that Sioux was also alert to what was going on and was moving to put herself between Adi and the onrushing figures.

The escalator jerked to a halt, and Adi realised there was another group of figures stood at the top by the exit. It appeared that Adi, Sioux and their newfound companions were caught in a pincer movement by this group of blades who did not look like they intended to wish them a good morning and invite them for a hearty breakfast.

Ched led the group to the top, and they found their exit barred with the figures behind them blocking off the route back down to the platform. Adi scanned the area, and there was no sign of any officials or security due to the lockdown although the vide cameras still appeared to be recording.

A tall, powerful-looking individual moved towards Ched who was tentatively trying to placate the person with his hands up in a gesture of friendship. Adi tapped the person next to him, "What the chuffing hades is going on? Who the fuck are these people?"

The man with Springett on his white tunic wiped his sweaty brow and whispered to Adi, "Not good, my friend, these blades are pushing their luck more and more, they want our electronic passes, makes it easier for them to go about their criminal activities."

Ched appeared to be making a point to the gang leader when he was struck by an almighty blow to the side of his head. Ched slumped to the floor, and the black-clad figure knelt beside him and ripped the electronic keypad from around his neck. His two colleagues quickly moved towards their stricken leader but backed off when a couple of the blades fronted them up with large, ferocious-looking machetes.

A squat figure approached them and in a strong Cathay accent said, "Stop there, unless you want the same as this sap," pointing at the prone Ched on the ground still writhing in agony.

"Hand over your passes and any spare credits you have, and we may let you leave intact, or we could do a few emergency amputations", he said in a threatening and mocking tone.

The two remaining humans and the three robots began to throw their electronic devices and a smattering of credits on the floor in front of the squat blade twirling his razor-sharp machete as if he was a cheerleader at an old-fashioned ball game.

Suddenly all the focus was on Adi and Sioux as they had nothing to hand over just being temporary members of the work detail. The squat thug moved menacingly towards them, flexing his forearm in a cutting motion.

"Don't try and hide behind that robot, freak, just hand it over. We know that all these robots are not allowed to hurt us so it can whistle and play with themselves."

The blades were aware of the legislation that forced robots to be fitted with failsafe devices that stopped them harming humans and even other robots if attacked or threatened.

The squat thug shoved Sioux aside and grabbed Adi by the front of his tunic, waving the machete by his right ear.

Adi stuttered, "I have nowt, they were doing me a favour, I'm not really part of this work detail, just leave it."

The squat thug with increasing malevolence spat at Adi and struck him with his free hand, laughing as he said to his audience of fellow blades, "About time we had a bit of gladiatorial sport, let the fun begin, eh guys and girls."

The work detail began backing away, and the blades gathered in a circle around Adi baying, shouting, and making a whooping sound.

Adi put his hands in the air trying to placate his attackers, attempting to reason with the now giggling, squat aggressor. He realised that he had nowhere to go; all his escape routes blocked. A thought flashed into his brain as if he had randomly tuned into a strange radiofrequency. Adi could not understand the communication, but despite the danger, he was in, everything suddenly became calm, and he was no longer frightened or apprehensive.

Sioux burst through the hollering blades knocking a couple of the thugs to the floor. She then confronted the squat one who was now waving his machete around. In a mocking tone, he squared up to Sioux, "What are you going to do to me - you bag of nuts, bolts and transistors - clear off and go and pick up some rubbish you robot nothing."

Adi was transfixed, convinced he could almost see a twinkle in Sioux's electronic eyes as she lifted her arm. Everything was a blur as a gleaming steel wire shot from the robotic arm in one lightning movement and sliced through the neck of the still laughing squat blade.

The cut was so fine that his head stayed on his shoulders, and it was only the red line of blood like a necklace that gave away that something was wrong. His body slumped to the ground, and his head rolled away to the top of the escalator. Sioux swivelled, and donkey kicked two of the nearest gang members who careered away to the far side of the room. The remainder of the blades backed off, looking totally shocked at the violent attack by a supposedly pacifist robot.

Sioux grabbed Adi and pulled him away from the headless body of the blade now pumping blood all over the floor. They moved towards the exit where Ched was now back on his feet and gathering his work detail around him.

CHAPTER SEVENTEEN

Adi and Sioux left through the station exit into an enclosed square, still empty due to the lockdown. They flattened themselves against the wall as a troop of shock militia ran into the station area alerted by reports of the disturbance. Adi could see them chasing the remaining members of the gang back down the escalator onto the platform.

Ched and the work detail had already started gathering up the parts of the blade's body and cleaning the blood from the floor of the concourse. Adi quickly gained his bearings and led the now subservient robot to the agreed meeting place. Adi looked at his time switch and realised despite the hassle he was still early for the agreed meet and still breathing thanks to his new robot companion.

An official politburo vehicle glided into the atrium, silently drawing to a halt in front of Adi and Sioux. Such transporters were rarely seen in this part of Steel City. Its presence soon began to draw the attention of the militia unit that was trying to piece together what had happened to the decapitated malcontent. Ched and his crew were quietly disappearing into the background and locating their "cleaning assignment."

Adi realised that Sioux was sending him a message as the words crackled painfully in his brain. Adi looked at Sioux who was as impassive as ever apart from the ever-present twinkle in her electronic eyes.

"Farewell, Citizen Newton, I have completed the task set me by Harry, and you are safe and delivered intact, apologies for the trouble, but there was no option. I need to return to Paradise. We may meet again one day. Goodbye, my love."

Adi's head throbbed as he received the parting words from Sioux and he looked in amazement at the departing android. The android sashayed through the militiamen who had rounded up the remaining members of the gang and were giving them a severe beating with their metal batons. Adi imagined they would soon be on transport to take them to The Killing Field.

Sioux reached the escalator and descended down to the platform to catch the next tram back to Harry Haslam.

The door to the transporter purred open, and Adi recognised the shaved head, seductive purple eyes and the red and green snake tattoo of Sabella. She beckoned him into the vehicle, and he sat in the seat next to her. A belt slid into place and secured him in the seat as the door shut and the transporter silently moved away from the transport hub area. The vehicle started travelling at speed through the still empty connecting corridors of Steel City.

Adi went to speak, but Sabella put up a jewelled encrusted hand covered in more snake tattoos, telling him to keep his counsel until they had arrived at their destination. The only other inhabitant was what looked like an android who was undertaking the steering duties. The vehicle had blacked out windows and Adi was unable to see anything of the checkpoints they encountered and each time after a few seconds, were given the approval to proceed.

Eventually, the transporter stopped, and the windows suddenly became transparent. Adi could see that they had pulled into a parking area lit brightly with floodlights and overseen by numerous vide cameras. The door opened, and with his restraints lifted, he clambered out followed by Sabella.

Sabella poked him in the back with her hand, and he could feel the crunch as her jewellery met his spine. She pointed in the direction of a lift in the corner of the parking space. Moving in the direction of the lift, they followed a dotted yellow line on the floor to keep them away from other vehicles that were coming and going.

Sabella whispered in his ear, "Don't look so frit Newton my boy, I will explain everything when we reach my workspace." Her voice was soothing and calm and lessened Adi's anxiety about what he was going to encounter next. Sabella placed her hand against the control panel, the doors opened, and she guided him in. The four walls were blank, and there did not seem to be any indication of floor numbering.

Sabella grinned at him, "The only way you can activate this lift is through personal contact if you are registered with the security system, and then you can only get out at the floor your clearance allows you to disembark. And don't think of chopping hands off or plucking eyeballs out as sensors can detect if you are living or not."

Adi looked bemused, "Never, why would people want to do that?"

Sabella looked serious for once and whispered, "It is amazing what the malcontents and rebels will do to try and get into this area to spread their poison." The lift door opened and Adi stepped out and tentatively followed Sabella who was gliding purposefully off to the right. She was pushing buttons on an entrance pad, and a thick steel door whizzed up and allowed them both through into a square box of a room with a large picture window at the far end. Outside the view looked out on to an unusually green landscape and a large number of statues.

Sabella took up position in a swivel chair surrounded by tabletops. These suddenly burst into life and began humming as she pushed buttons and tapped a keyboard displayed on the monitor that had appeared from the far edge of the desk in front of her. She gestured for Adi to sit down as a tall backed chair seemed to move of its own volition and settled on the other side of the desk from the now distracted Sabella.

Adi sat down, still bewildered at the chair that moved by itself. He became aware that the chair was adjusting to fit the contours of his body and changing the height so that his feet were in the perfect position to make him comfortable.

Sabella glanced up grinning again, "Expect you have never encountered the latest ergonomic seating design, adjusts itself to give you the perfect posture but eh, don't piss it off as it can make life very uncomfortable for you."

Adi smiled weakly, not knowing if he should take Sabella seriously but decided he didn't really want to find out. Adi looked around the room and said, "Is this where the Maskirovka are based then? Where's the rest of your crew, Zaf and Anton, who saved me on my way to Paradise?"

Sabella sat up straight and glared at Adi, the black and red snake entwined on her neck and face almost seemed to be hissing at him.

"Look Citizen Newton, Cyd or Adi whatever you want to be called today, be careful what you say and when you say it, you are here to help us, don't start asking stupid questions. The Maskirovka is a top-secret, clandestine organisation; we operate on a need to know basis, the only elite official who is aware of our mission is Woodward. We try and keep her at arm's length as we are never really sure what her agenda is from day to day, you listening Cyd, my boy?"

Adi put his hands in the air in a conciliatory gesture and tensed up as his chair seemed to be squeezing him, and it was starting to feel uncomfortable. "Sorry, just call me Cyd and keep this damn chuffing chair under control. I know I have no choice and I keep being told to do what I am told but frankly no one is telling me what I need to do."

A screen appeared in front of Adi projecting a picture of several faces. He recognised some of them as members of the elite Nomenklatura butchered in the honey traps. Sabella interjected and said, "Yes, there are more who have fallen into the trap, thinking more of their groins than their scrawny necks."

Sabella continued, "Thanks to your work in Paradise and making contact with Harry Haslam we now have a concrete lead on the group who appear to be behind these attacks. We had tried for a long time to get into contact with him, but he blocked us from all angles, I think he thought we wanted to detain him and send him off to The Killing Field".

Sabella smiled, but the red and black snake still seemed to be glowering at him, "Well done, Cyd, you achieved what Woodward wanted you to do, she has always seemed very keen to track down Harry but now wants no action taken against him. No accounting for the machinations of those in charge."

"You and I are accompanying a militia unit later as thanks to Harry we have been made aware of an attack planned to take place this evening. We hope to catch them in the act and eradicate this problem once and for all."

Adi sat up, his senses working on overtime, pleased that he had achieved one objective in liaising with Ha Ha Harry and was good to now be involved in the potential capture of the group bumping off members of the Nomenklatura.

Adi went to speak, but Sabella put her hand up to stop him. "It could be a long evening, you need to get some rest, take these." She handed him a fistful of little green tablets and pointed him to a hatch that was opening on the wall with a vibra bed inside. "Get some sleep; I will make sure you are called ready for the operation tonight, sweet dreams, Cyd, dear boy."

Adi was pleased to leave the ergonomic chair, slugged the tablets back and settled down on the vibra bed. The tablets took immediate effect, and he was asleep as soon as he laid down.

Sabella strolled over and checked that Adi was unconscious before she lithely pirouetted back to her desk and at once tapping again at the keys on her screen. The vibra bed moved and a skull cap attached itself to Adi's head, and laser probes began slithering into different regions of his brain. Arm and leg restraint snapped into place to ensure he was not able to struggle if he awoke.

Sabella stared at the picture of Adi's brain, which now appeared in front of her, showing the probes as they slowly moved around the various parts of his cranium. "Sorry, Cyd, had to be done, old chap."

PART TWO: THE SECRET LIFE OF THE STATION OF THE MIND

CHAPTER EIGHTEEN

Sabella manipulated the green snaking lines as they travelled around Adi's brain; the first task was to locate the "Healthy Life" chip implanted in his teenage years during his time at Hawking College. She carefully isolated the chip and turned if off simultaneously sending a fine laser light into the area to destroy it without a trace.

Sabella breathed a huge sigh of relief that she had undertaken this without any hitch, a fraction of an ell either way and Newton's mind would be cooked mush. Sabella had undergone years of training to be able to work with such intricate technological equipment, only one of a number approved within the whole of Steel City. She had even been seconded to other areas of the country to undertake similar tasks involving important security matters.

Sabella did not undertake this work for health or humanitarian reasons but to unlock secrets and memories hidden away in the subject's minds. Once she had vaporised the inserted chip, she started a programme which at ultra-high speed re-ran the whole life of the subject and allowed her via the attached scanner to extract and isolate important information. Sabella set the process in motion with a great deal of trepidation; she was aware that there was a high attrition rate with a third of all subjects never recovering to reach a conscious state trapped in a looped dream dominated existence. She knew she could not afford to lose Newton as she was aware that Woodward wanted him delivered to her alive when the process was complete.

Adi jerked into consciousness, but it was as if he was observing himself participating in one of his vivid dreams. He was unable to feel or move his body, but he grimaced in his sleep as he felt a sudden, sharp, searing pain in his head, which just as quickly disappeared. Adi settled into a tranquil, meditative state as his favourite Clock DVA tracks played as background music.

Sabella smiled as she clicked on a drop-down box of anarchistic, anachronistic, old fashioned music tracks. She then selected those indicated on her screen as the subject's favourites, Clock DVA, De Tian, Cocktail Party and Disease. "Wow", she sneered. "Dull as dull can be."

Adi could feel his heart slowing to the funereal beat of "Buried Dreams" by Clock DVA, it felt like he was in the best seat in the house for the cinema show of his life. He looked around for a tonic drink and sugar treats but realised there was nothing there.

The show had been rolling for about dvadtsat minut when Adi realised he was sobbing as he watched his early life unfold before him. These memories had been blocked or erased in his teenage years; it was painful being reminded of what he had gone through and who was involved.

Sabella was watching the same cinema show on her screen and looked stunned at the unfolding events and sent a terse mail message to Woodward with the news that what she now knew would put her on high alert and changed all their plans.

For the first time, Adi knew something about his parents and how he came to be placed in the care of the state at a very early age. He was soon enrolled onto the fast-track Hawking programme to serve the interests of the state. However, it was clear that as Adi grew older, he developed a rebellious streak and began to kick against the system and became a major irritant to the overseers at Hawking College.

"Corrective Treatment" merged into "Repression" from the late seventies Sheffield band Disease as his heart sped up in line with the accelerating beat of the accompanying music. Adi began to watch in horror as he was sent to live in a special wing of the Hawking College and began to realise what was happening to him and other young people who lived there.

Sabella also began to stare at her screen with trepidation as she watched several of the Nomenklatura visit the young people and with help from the staff physically and sexually abuse them. It was clear that Adi was targeted regularly and threatened with dire consequences if he told anyone although there wasn't anyone to tell.

Adi squirmed with disgust as he watched and recalled the treatment he had been subjected to, and how he had repressed these savage memories for many years. He sensed he was listening to "Touch Sensitivity" which merged into "Seventh Heaven" from De Tian as he forced the bile down as the anger spread through his body and he craved retribution.

Sabella was taking notes of the names of the visitors who were abusing the Hawking students and realised most of them were on the list of executed elite politburo members. It seemed no coincidence then that they were being slaughtered. But who was behind these criminal acts? They must have a connection with the students who had been abused. Sabella manipulated the probes in Adi's brain, and he fell into a deep, unthinking coma, the cinema show of his life halted as his body was showing signs of extreme distress. This also allowed Sabella to start undertaking some investigations into the potential perpetrators of the string of murders.

Sabella frowned as she started identifying other students who had been subjected to abuse at Hawking College and checked where they were now living and working. After a while, it dawned on her that they had a major problem that needed sorting with immediate effect. She called Woodward.

After several vide calls Sabella returned to the connection to Adi Newton's brain, she lit the green probes on her screen again and began adjusting the awareness level. Adi began sparking back to a semi-conscious state. The cinema show of his life resumed, and Adi was again watching scenes from his life and thankfully for his wellbeing the subject was his latter years. Apart from a couple of short-lived relationships, a few failed investigations and the attack that left him scarred, everything was on an even keel.

Sabella fiddled with her personal retro music collection and decided to subject Adi to one of her favourite groups, a Caledonian combo from Glasweegie called Mogwai. She selected a couple of tracks from the "Come On Die Young" set starting with "Waltz with Aidan" and "May Nothing but Happiness come through your Door."

She chuckled at her private joke then sat back and waited for the cinema show to run its course. She could then start the delicate process of resuscitating Citizen Newton, knowing full well how vital it was that she achieved this without any problems. She knew her career, and even her life depended on her success.

Adi began to wake up and felt like he had the hangover from hell, too much sugar, moonshine and black-market drugs all at once. Adi's head throbbed, and he had a general feeling of doom and desperation. With his many thoughts and memories twisted together, he began the task of unscrambling them and make some sense of what had gone on while he thought he was just having a nap. And what was that dreadful, discordant music playing in the background?

Sabella moved from her work station and greeted Adi as he staggered from his sleeping berth.

"Dazed and confused, dear boy, that was a deep and illuminating slumber, you need to come and sit at my desk, and we need to have a serious discussion about what has gone on, and we need to take action very soon, eh Cyd or as I know you better now, will call you Adi, ok boy."

His whole body ached as he dragged himself across the room and remade acquaintance with the ergonomic chair, which, to his surprise, appeared sympathetic and began gently massaging his aching limbs.

Adi struggled to speak, every syllable crashing around in his head. "What the chuffing hell happened? Feels like I a celestial comet has hit me and what were those effing tablets you gave me, Sabella? Why does my head hurt so much and I feel like gipping?"

Sabella, looked sympathetic, with the red and black snake even appearing to be eyeing him benignly. Sabella sparked a two-way screen to life so that they both could see what information she was punching in via her cyber bracelet. A list of names appeared in front of Adi. "Ashton Lukashenko", "Count Salman

Mubarak", "Ivan Starikov", "Vladimir Stankovich" and "Trenton Pariknov."

Sabella said, "Do you recognise any of these names?" Adi shook his still pounding head. "I'll put some pictures up of these characters, see if you recognise any of them?"

Adi looked at the screen in horror; all of the men were frighteningly familiar. He looked at them one by one over and over again. Adi attempted to persuade himself that he did not know them, but it just made his head pulse with more pain. Tears rolled down his cheeks, his whole body began convulsing, and he felt the need to be sick.

Sabella moved around her desk to stand in front of him and gave him a handful of orange tablets. She squeezed his shoulder, and a feeling of warmth and calm began to course through his body as he swallowed the tablets in one go.

Sabella moved back to her desk and looked at Adi with a concerned gaze. "We do not have enough time to fully explain what has happened, but the bottom line is that these so-called elite politburo members were part of a paedophile group that abused scholars at Hawking College. We unlocked the buried secrets of your mind, and it is now clear why all these members of the Nomenklatura were targeted and eliminated - painfully. We are now sure that some of your fellow ex-students have waged a campaign to seek retribution for you and other abused students."

Adi looked dumbstruck but had now gained control of his emotions and thoughts. It struck him how glad he was that this unknown group of people were punishing these evil bastards. Adi knew there were still others who had been involved and felt a strong desire to pay them back for the anguish and suffering he and others had undergone.

Sabella continued talking, "Thanks to your new friend, Harry Haslam, we know that one of the elite politburo is planning to visit a courtesan called Su Xiao Xiao tonight in the Star City complex. He will be intercepted, kidnapped and eliminated. He is a very prominent and long-standing politician, and we understand one of the leaders of the paedophile group. Do you recognise him?"

Adi began to feel angry as he looked at the image and recalled the most brutal of the abusers, a large, sweaty, malodorous man with jagged teeth.

"Is that Sir Cyrille Lishavsky? He was the vilest of the lot. Are we going to save him or finish him off?"

Sabella looked perplexed. "Officially we are supposed to be stopping the killings but given what we now know how can we justify allowing a perverted low life like Lishavsky to get away and be free to carry on abusing, eh Adi, my friend?" she said.

"I have a plan that will hopefully, as they say, kill two birds with one rock; we need to unmask the renegades who are undertaking these executions. I have looked at past lists of Hawking College students who also lived in the residential unit, and I have come up with some interesting names of those who may have the resources and enough anger to carry out these acts of revenge but exposing them may prove difficult."

"Get your act together Newton we are off to Star City, let us see who we can track down and put an end to this lawlessness. We can also expose this paedophile group, well those that are left, eh Adi?"

CHAPTER NINETEEN

Adi brushed himself down and followed Sabella to the door that emerged in the far wall and led to the lift area. Sabella activated the control panel, and they entered the brightly lit elevator and descended at speed to floor zero where they came to an abrupt halt. They left the elevator, and Sabella pointed the way to an escalator which ferried them to a transit area heavily guarded by the black-clad militia.

A group immediately confronted them and began checking them over with an electronic device. Sabella showed them an identification pass and some further information on her screen as she pointed at Adi. Three of the militia separated themselves from the main group and made it clear that Sabella and Adi were to follow them.

Sabella whispered to Adi, "Just do as they say, we are all off to Star City."

"Ok, not going to argue, snake lady," replied Adi.

Sabella glared at him, with the red and black snake tattoo almost hissing at him. They followed the trio of militia to an exit out to a shaded rooftop. Adi was stunned as they were escorted to a bright red gyrocopter. As far as he was aware, these were firmly based in history, and he did not realise that they existed anymore.

The five of them climbed on board, and the pilot nodded at them as they strapped themselves in. The machine started up with a very quiet thrum, and warning lights flashed on the display in front of their seats. Adi screwed up his eyes as the gyrocopter took to the air and began skimming across the buildings, to the left was Paradise, The Killing Field and then desolate parched ground with ruins at irregular intervals as far as he could see.

Sabella tapped frantically on her cyber bracelet trying to get hold of her Maskirovka colleagues Zaf and Anton to coordinate with them about the planned action that evening. Adi remained spellbound as the machine flew over the modern apartments and luxury entertainment and commercial areas where the privileged worked, lived and played. They neared the outlying area of Star City a halfway settlement involving many older retired members of the elite and the nursery blocks where all children were brought up communally.

CHAPTER TWENTY

Sir Cyrille Lishavsky waddled down the brightly lit corridor leading from his luxury apartment and clicked his fingers at the two hefty heavily armed figures dressed in green, their faces obscured by protective helmets. These two females were from the 'Green Warriors, a private security company favoured by the mega-rich and influential. They were allowed to carry lethal weapons and trained in the full range of offensive martial arts.

Sir Cyrille was visiting Star City to see his favoured courtesan Su Xiao Xiao, a transgender person trapped in her pre-pubescent teens by extreme chemical intervention. Sir Cyrille knew well some of his erstwhile colleagues had been brutally executed and he was taking all necessary precautions for his visit.

CHAPTER TWENTY-ONE

The gyrocopter gently landed on the giant X on top of the local government building on the edge of Star City. The group disembarked quickly from their airconditioned transport, broiling briefly in the 120 gradusov temperature before ducking their way into the cool sanctity of the control room of the local government militia of Star City.

Sabella greeted a tall, thin man of about sem futov, who spoke with an affected cultured accent who ushered her and Adi into a side room. The three militia guards stood outside the door as it closed and gave out hostile looks to the curious eyes of the local officials.

The tall, thin man introduced himself as Captain Bassett, before motioning for them all to sit down and handing them beakers of high-quality coffee bean liquor. He raised his cup and said, "Good felicitations to you on your mission; we will endeavour to give you support if you so require."

Sabella acknowledged the gesture and raised her beaker and tapped it against Adi's cup and said,

"Thank you, Captain Bassett, we believe we have the situation covered, but please be on alert if you are required. We are tracking our person of interest and he should be arriving within the hour. We will take your leave but thank you for the welcome and hospitality."

Sir Cyrille Lishavsky and his two Green Warrior guards approached the area of Star City where Su Xiao Xiao's apartment pod was located. They were on high alert, but they did not see the two figures surreptitiously following them through the busy corridors of Star City. These hooded figures were aware this was Sir Cyrille Lishavsky, their target. They also knew that his bodyguards were highly trained and would need to be dealt with carefully.

Sabella was still trying to get hold of her colleagues, Zaf and Anton for back up. They were not answering and were either busy on a project or more worryingly purposely ignoring her. Sabella beckoned to Adi, and they said their farewells to Captain Bassett and flanked by the three militia guards they set off through the busy corridors to make their way to the apartment pod of Su Xiao Xiao.

Su Xiao Xiao readied herself for her impending visitor ingesting a handful of pills to deaden the pain of having to submit to such a disgusting odious pervert like Cyrille. The only consolation was that he paid well and of course, he was so unfit he did not last too long.

Su looked forward to visiting the designer shops later to spend the money she would earn, which would be scant recompense for the ordeal she was about to endure. Su put on some background music to prepare herself mentally for the visit, "One Step More and You Die" by Mono, a Nihonese instrumental band.

Sir Cyrille and his two protectors neared the apartment pod of Su Xiao Xiao. They did not make a move towards the entrance until they were sure everything was clear. The taller of the two guards rang the intercom, and when the door was open, she pushed her way in past a startled Su. The guard undertook a thorough search of the apartment and remained impassive when she found the bondage room with chains, restraints, and a spiked bed along with lots of other weird and painful-looking objects.

The guard emerged and nodded to her colleague that everything was clear. An impatient Sir Cyrille pushed his way in followed by the courtesan, Su. The taller guard ensured the entrance was secure and allowed herself a smile as she said to her colleague, "No accounting for taste, I hope she is being paid well for satisfying that obese freak."

The second guard shifted her position to be able to see anyone approaching the apartment block. She turned to give her own unfavourable opinion of Sir Cyrille, but before she was able to speak, a flash of brilliant, white light illuminated them both, and they were immediately paralyzed and fell to the floor.

The two hooded figures rushed up to them. The first one, a huge, physical presence, frisked them and removed their laser weapons, sabre knives and communication devices. The second hooded figure bent down and whispered to the still mentally aware guards, "We are not going to harm you, but you will be dumped a long way away from here, and your paralysis will wear off by sunset. Your only problem will be having to explain to your bosses how you were outwitted so easily, dorks."

The smaller hooded figure clicked her fingers, and three dark uniformed robots appeared who then secured the guard's hands and legs with ties. They heaved them into a large refuse collection bin and quickly made tracks through the crowds pushing their human cargo to the agreed destination.

Sir Cyrille was angry, how dare these low life pipsqueaks try to threaten him and other members of the Nomenklatura. They were nothing, and if he found any of them, they would be on a fast-track journey to The Killing Field. He entered the bondage room, and Su looked at him and asked, "Zhu Lishavsky, what is your wish today, and can I check you will be depositing the agreed credits in my account."

Sir Cyrille exploded and struck Su straight in her face, her studded nose exploding with green blood. "How dare you, don't question me, you are nothing better than the vermin who live in the ruins."

Su curled up in a ball as Sir Cyrille started kicking her with his large booted foot, and who by now was so enraged he was spitting at her. Su was unable to speak, she had never known him to be this violent, and she would need all her experience to get out of this situation without further punishment.

The smaller hooded figure was working on the door lock with her electronic picklock. She soon found the correct code and the door opened, they burst in and followed the noise of crying and shouting. They located the room where the racket was coming from and found themselves confronted by a large, sweaty man kicking and punching the prone, slight figure of Su who was squirming away trying to minimize the impact of the blows from her demented aggressor. Sir Cyrille was so out of it that he did not notice the two hooded figures come into the room and stand behind him.

Both of the hooded figures drew laser pencils and pointed them at Sir Cyrille who continued to kick the screaming Su.

"You fat pervert fuck, leave her alone", said the smaller of the two. The bigger hooded figure moved between Sir Cyrille and Su, swiftly striking him with a hefty kick between the legs. Sir Cyrille fell to the floor like a deflated balloon and began making a high pitched, squealing noise.

Both of the hooded figures stood over Sir Cyrille and removed their disguises, "Remember us, you probably don't as we were just two of the many you abused, but we certainly are unable to forget you. Stop whining, pervert, you are going to have a lot more to complain about before we are finished."

The larger male figure, who had remained silent so far, reached down and grabbed the now snivelling Sir Cyrille by the neck and with enormous strength lifted him off his feet and slammed his massive bulk into the wall. Sir Cyrille slid down to the floor, the large, powerful man pulled his head up by the hair and in a swift movement sliced off his large podgy, veined left ear.

"Ve vill be chopping off other parts of yur disgusting body, ya bastard." The large, muscular figure bent down and started undoing the belt on Sir Cyrille's voluminous trousers as he brandished his razor-sharp scalpel.

Sir Cyrille started screaming, "Leave me alone, I'll give you anything you want if you let me go," His chubby hand was trying to stem the flow of the black blood pumping from where his ear had been. "You can have all the credits you want" he stuttered, "Please, I am sorry for what I did to you."

The three of them had forgotten Su who was now standing and holding a towel to her profusely bleeding nose. Unnoticed, she quickly moved towards Sir Cyrille and jabbed a finger into his left eye socket. As she withdrew her finger the eye came away with a sucking sound. The dagger-like point of her nail glistened with the innards of Lishavsky's eyeball. Su smiled and walked away.

Sir Cyrille was writhing on the floor trying to stop the muscular man undoing his belt and taking his trousers off. He was fighting a losing battle and before long Sir Cyrille was naked from the waist down. The powerful man flexed his arm and readied his already bloodied scalpel to further disfigure Sir Cyrille. His huge, bloated belly-flopped on the floor as he squirmed to turn over in an attempt to protect himself.

CHAPTER TWENTY-TWO

None of the four people in the flat was aware as the lock on the door splintered as Adi levered it open with a steel bar, realising they did not have enough time to pick it electronically. Sabella rushed in followed by Adi both holding laser weapons which they pointed at the melee of bodies entwined before them.

Their militia escort stood guard on the door while the back up for the hooded duo were now secured with electronic wrist ties and seated against the wall. Several citizens going about their daily business were ushered away from the area with one of the militiamen using a stun gun on one rubbernecker who had attempted to take a vid to upload on social news.

Sir Cyrille was still rolling around on the floor screaming for help when suddenly his two assailants stopped struggling with him as they realised Sabella and Adi had them covered with their weapons.

Sabella shook her head, the black and red snake seeming to spit disapproval at the two figures in front of her. Knowing they were outflanked, the renegades threw their laser weapons and blades to the ground.

Sabella angrily exclaimed at them, "No wonder I couldn't get hold of you, it was you two all along executing these members of the elite politburo. How could you, yes you... I am speechless."

Adi realised that Sabella was expressing her anger at her two colleagues from The Maskirovka that he had met earlier, Zaf and Anton. Adi responded to a gesture from Sabella and moved towards the duo and placed electronic handcuffs on them, forcing them to stand back to back. Sabella also threw him some ankle restraints that she had spotted in Su's bondage room collection.

Adi then began to examine Su's injuries and gave her some pain killer to dull the pain and helped her clear the green blood from her face. Su then staggered to the galley area and poured herself a long drink of something presumably illegal and packed full of stimulants.

Sabella hauled Sir Cyrille to his feet, black blood clots had begun to form over the clean cut wound where his ear once sat, and he was holding his eye which was oozing a jelly-like green liquid. He started shouting at Sabella, "Where have you been, you should have arrived earlier, you will both be on a charge of dereliction of duty. You could be even joining these two on a one-way trip to The Killing Field. Give me a blade I want revenge on these low lives now and that worthless whore."

Sabella propelled Sir Cyrille towards a low divan and pushed him down, "Stay there, Sir Cyrille, I need to speak to these two myself."

He made to get up, but Adi with a look of disgust on his face pushed him back down with a hand to the chest and waved his laser weapon under his nose. Adi whispered, "Don't push me; I know who you are."

Sabella confronted her erstwhile colleagues who looked shamefaced as she gesticulated at them, "How dare you put the Maskirovka in danger, how is this going to look when Woodward and the top security realise that the threat has come from within? To be honest, I feared this as soon as I saw your names as ex-students at Hawking College and lived in the residential accommodation. I presume Fat Cyrille here, and his pervert friends abused you as well?"

Anton, despite his huge frame and fearsome appearance, was crying, tears cascading down his cheeks and despite trying was unable to speak. Zaf still appeared defiant, and her pixie-like face twisted with hatred as she spat in the direction of Sir Cyrille, still prevented from standing by Adi.

"You don't know what he and his friends used to do to us, no one cared, and someone had to do something. We supposedly live in a modern, civilized society, not like the brutal days of our ancestors, are you happy that our alleged leaders can abuse our children without any comeback?"

Sabella looked at Adi before replying, "I do know what happened, I watched what happened to Adi here when I was able to access his buried dreams. Sick behaviour, from people who should know better. But how can I condone what you and Anton have been doing murdering people even if you had a good reason? What are we going to do about it eh?"

Adi started to speak, "Will we need to contact Woodward? We need to check with her...."

Sabella barked, "Be quiet Newton, this is my decision alone; I am in charge here, ok boy!"

Sir Cyrille piped up, "Well done, call up some reinforcements and get these villains into custody, we can try them quickly and get them off to The Killing Field pretty damn rapid, eh snake face? And while you're at it book a cell for this no-good bitch whore as well, how dare they attack a man of my standing, she can suffer as well, low life degenerates, all of them!"

Sabella looked in horror at Sir Cyrille and mumbled, "Yes sir, certainly sir, will jump to it."

Zaf and Anton looked shamefaced as they awaited their fate, knowing full well that any trial was in name only and that Sir Cyrille would ensure any moderators would do his bidding and condemn them to execution. Zaf went to speak, but Sabella silenced her with a wave of her arm.

Sabella looked at Adi, "Get Sir Cyrille ready to travel, sort his belt and trousers out and clean up his face, give the man the dignity his reputation deserves." Adi helped Sir Cyrille adjust his trousers over his huge stomach and with a cloth and cream from the galley cleaned his face and bathed his wounds.

Sir Cyrille brayed, "Careful you oaf, or you'll be up on a charge as well!" Adi moved behind the obese Sir Cyrille and at a sign from Sabella grabbed both his wrists and shackled them with electronic handcuffs. "What the deuce do you think you are doing you...."

Sir Cyrille was open-mouthed like a landed fish gasping for air as he watched Sabella free Zaf and Anton who moved towards Sir Cyrille.

Sabella spat her words out with venom, "Zaf and Anton have given me their oath that this will be their last kidnap and execution. There will be no more. I am afraid Sir Cyrille you need to pay for your evil misdeeds, I have ordered them not to treat you well before they finish you off."

Adi grinned and slapped Sir Cyrille on the back of his sweaty head, and as he tried to protest, he gagged him with the bloody cloth he had used to clean him up earlier. Zaf and Anton took Sir Cyrille by his pudgy arms and propelled him out of the door before Sabella could change her mind. Adi had removed Sir Cyrille's security belt and all his credits and lobbed them towards Su Xiao Xiao, "Hopefully, this will recompense you and help you forget what happened today."

Su, "Thank you, what did happen today?" she said with her yellow eyes twinkling, "All forgotten, thanks again," as she winked and handed Adi one of her contact cards.

Sabella called after Zaf and Anton, "Don't worry about the security vide, Captain Bassett has made sure nothing will be picked up until I give him the nod. Meet me in my office pod at zakat solntsa tonight, don't be late and make sure you clean up properly after you."

Adi looking perplexed asked Sabella, "Sir Cyrille's guards didn't put up much of a fight, thought those Green Warriors were the best and not to be messed with?"

Sabella responded with a wry smile on her face, "You don't know who their ultimate leader is, do you? Our dear friend Woodward, and they were under strict orders. Time to go, Newton, for we need to catch up with Woodward and discuss what happens next."

As they left the apartment Su Xiao Xiao cranked up the volume on her surround-sound music system and "Barbarism Begins at Home" by the long-forgotten band, The Smiths resounded as Su hugged herself and danced.

PART THREE: SUMMER IS A COMING IN

CHAPTER TWENTY-THREE

Adi and Sabella entered through the security barrier having been electronically frisked by two Green Warriors. They then escorted them to an elevator where they were met at the top and searched again. Finally, they were ushered into a large office where Woodward was sitting behind a gleaming metallic desk.

Woodward waved them in and gestured for them to sit down on two seats set up in front of her. A faceless android placed two drinks on the desk in front of them and moved to stand guard on the door.

Woodward addressed her guests, "Mission accomplished, well done both of you, we have now eliminated all of the paedophiles who were members of the elite politburo. I am sure you are pleased about that Newton. We have weakened the establishment

111

and now need to finish the job. Zaf and Anton can now set in action our next phase of the plan. Sabella, make sure everything is coordinated and no mistakes."

Woodward now concentrated her steely gaze on Adi, "I am pleased I put my faith in you, Newton to help us through this wretched conundrum. I am not sure you knew what you were doing half the time, but you blundered through with the support and guidance of Sabella here, be pleased for the moment, Newton but there is further work to do."

"I want you to accompany Sabella to meet with the other members of the Maskirovka and be appraised of what happens next. We need to give you an idea of the current political situation here in Steel City and how this fits in globally."

Sabella picked up the conversation, "Our actions have been a double-edged sword, we have rid the metropolis of an evil cabal of abusers who have been free to commit serious crimes with no worries. Secondly, we have seriously weakened the grip of the ruling elite, and we are now in a position to overthrow them and bring about new democratic leadership in Steel City."

Adi pondered what he was being told, and of the many questions he could have asked he started with," And who the hell is this new regime and who is going to lead them?"

Woodward frowned and glared at Adi, "Don't get ahead of yourself Newton, all will be revealed in good time, don't worry, you will have an important role to play."

A faceless android moved away from the door which noiselessly opened. Woodward indicated to Sabella and Adi that their audience was now over, and it was time to leave. They were escorted to the elevator, and from there Adi followed Sabella through a maze of corridors and escalators before they arrived at a nondescript building with a sign on the front saying it was a Tuning Fork Factory.

Sabella ushered Adi into the foyer and through security, and they took a lift to the top floor. The building was old, but the highest stop on the lift led out into an ultra-modern open plan office. Sabella walked the length of the room and opened a reinforced door with an electronic key card. They entered a small office and sat down at an oblong desk fitted with computer terminals. They were immediately followed into the workspace by Zaf and Anton who quietly sat down and logged on to the terminals in front of them.

Sabella suddenly clapped her hands above her head and started singing.

"Life, strife- those two are one

Naught can ye win but by faith and daring

Firm in reliance, laugh a defiance

Laugh in hope for sure is the end

March, March, many as one

Shoulder to shoulder and friend to friend."

Sabella finished and banged her hands on the desk, "Listen to those words everyone, we are close to achieving our goal, we need to overthrow the old guard, wise words from Ethel Smyth a very long time ago."

Adi looked up," Nah then, what happens next, who are we overthrowing and why and how?"

Zaf and Anton at a signal from Sabella began speaking to various people on their communication devices. Sabella motioned for Adi to follow her and they entered an adjoining room with a large desk filled with computer equipment and a vast screen which filled the whole of the far wall. "I need you to be in contact with your friend Harry Haslam, you both have work to do, you need to work through the list now appearing on the screen and disable their communications and any security measures they have in place. Also please liaise with Captain Bassett as we need all CCVid cameras closed off in certain areas and contact channels between all the militia units disrupted. Think you are up to that Hawking boy?"

Adi replied," Ok boss snake woman, will do, and what are you and your two pals going to be doing?"

Sabella stood up straight and looked Adi directly in the eyes," We have waited and planned this for many years, Zaf and Anton have weakened the upper echelon of the ruling politburo. You may have noticed they are all men or were born men, and they have treated women as the lower class for too long.

Since the Sino-Sovok takeover many years ago they have used and exploited the people and resources of Steel City. We are fighting back; we have a significant number of Green Warriors and various sections of the militia and we will be taking out all the remaining members of the politburo leadership. Woodward is coordinating the whole putsch, and we will be installing a new supreme leader. Everything will be carried out smoothly so that the ordinary people in areas like Paradise will not know that anything has changed until we start improving the lives of all within Steel City."

Adi sat at the desk open-mouthed, unable to respond, shell-shocked at what he had heard. Sabella began to leave the room and looked back over her shoulder, "Don't just sit there like a drowning man, get fucking on with it, we will be touch, just make sure you and Harry do what we have asked, ok boy."

The vast screen filled with a link to Harry, who was flanked by his two guardian androids, Sioux and Patti. Adi greeted his friend, "Cracking to see you, Ha Ha and my saviour Sioux, looks like we had better get weaving and do as we have been asked. Sabella and the others have just left."

Harry responded, "Yes, my friend, looks like we have no choice and will be good to please my mother for once in my life!"

Adi scrolled through his stored tracks and latched onto a really old set of tunes he had not listened to for a long time but seemed to match the urgent mood. An ancient Steel City band called Molodoy crashed out "Death's Doll" and "Fix Your Face." Harry put his thumb up and said, "Let's do it, pal!"

PART FOUR: CODA/CHANGE OF THE GUARD

CHAPTER TWENTY-FOUR

Adi wiped his brow and slugged back another sugar shot; it appeared as if their mission was accomplished. Harry and Adi had cracked open the security system for the whole of the politburo and had begun to watch groups of Green Warriors rounding up the Sovoks and their staff. The majority of the Nomenklatura militia had been eliminated, unwittingly led into traps by Adi and Harry who were able to manipulate their commands and communications.

Adi stretched and yawned, a night of concentration and high-tech wizardry had taken its toll. He looked up at the feed and Harry seemed to be nodding off but was being kept awake by a vigilant Patti standing by his side.

They had been swapping tunes all night and Adi selected something to keep them buzzing and pumped. "Kebab Traume" boomed out by Deutsch Amerikanishe Freundschaft an anarchic blast of industrial noise. Suddenly the screen went dark and then Woodward appeared. "Thank you, gentlemen, your help was invaluable, apart from a few rogue groups of loyal militias we have neutralized all members of the elite politburo and their supporters. Can you both make your way to our new headquarters at Hillsborough House, we need to decide what happens next. Sabella will forward electronic passes to get you past The Green Warriors. Make haste, boys."

Woodward disappeared from the screen and Adi and Harry exchanged inquisitive glances as their communication was restored. Harry looked at Adi and thinking quickly said, "We will meet you at Leadmill, we can then find our way to Hillsborough House from there. Hopefully, it will be less traumatic than the last time you were there." Sioux appeared on the screen, and Adi looked twice as it appeared he was being winked at. "Haha, hopefully, no one loses their head this time, haha!", said Harry.

Adi gathered his gear together, and a message pinged in from Sabella with an electronic bar code to get him through any security barriers and checkpoints.

A black-suited android guard appeared and guided Adi to the lift and then led him along a maze of corridors and through a security door and he was at the Mark Hurst Transit Stop. Adi studied the map to check the journey details to get to Leadmill.

The platform was relatively empty, many residents of all areas staying at home as they sensed that something was happening, and it could be dangerous to be out in the open. Adi did not have to wait long before the tram arrived, and he boarded to travel the six stops to Leadmill. He received a message from Harry to say that he was on his way and would see him at Leadmill.

Harry and his two faithful androids started to make their way out of their pod, this being the first time they had ventured outside for a very long time. Harry gliding along in his hoverchair was getting strange looks from the locals of Paradise. They were not used to seeing someone with a disability in a public space as they were usually eliminated at birth or kept in secure institutions. Sioux and Patti made sure none of the curious residents managed to get too close to Harry.

They left the market area and joined the queue for the Tuk tram platform, creating a buzz of conversation amongst the waiting crowds. Rumours were already circulating about events in the restricted areas of Steel City and that some sort of insurrection was taking place. The general view was that nothing much would change and that they would still be paid little, overworked, and still have to live in terrible conditions.

Adi kicked his heels on Leadmill station waiting for Harry to arrive but made sure he kept away from where the previous trouble had erupted. There seemed to be a general air of excitement as people clamoured for news of what was going on, with speculation that there was going to be a city-wide compulsory newscast soon. Many people were gathering in the nearby Cossack Square anticipating an announcement soon.

CHAPTER TWENTY-FIVE

A tram pulled in on the platform below, and a large number of people made their way up to the exit area. Adi anxiously searched the crowd for Harry and his robotic guardians. They did not appear, so Adi checked the time of the next arrival. However, his attention was drawn to a commotion coming from the direction of the rarely used steps up from the platform. He wandered over and in the middle of the throng was Harry with Patti and Sioux either side of him. They were surrounded by a jeering group of blades pointing and shouting abuse at Harry.

Adi pushed his way through the gang, assessing how many there were and what danger they posed to Harry. Sioux moved towards him and sent him a mental message, "Stay chilled, under control."

Harry fronted up a tall, thin blade dressed in red and black who his friends were calling Sharp and urging him to "do the freak." Harry kept saying, "This is your last chance, fuck off pig, haha!"

Blade pulled out a large curved knife and slashed at Harry who manoeuvred his hoverchair and appeared behind his assailant. Harry lifted a small rectangular object, and a flash lightning struck Blade on the back of his neck, and he lit up with phosphorescent light, shook violently and began writhing on the floor. Sioux and Patti crashed into four of the gang and knocked them to the ground. Adi grabbed the oldest looking gang member and held him up by his throat.

"I assume you are the boss man, big boy, I suggest you take what is left of your sad, nesh mob and scoot before you get in real big trouble, you don't really want to know who you have just tried to assault."

The blades picked up their stricken gang member and disappeared out of the exit at high speed. Adi high fived Harry, and they moved towards the exit and made for the entrance of the transit system reserved for Hallam Village only. They logged in with the electronic passes that Sabella had provided and passed the Green Warriors at the security gate and made for the platform.

Harry said, "Good job we got you through that, need to get you to Woodward in one piece or else I will be in trouble again, haha!"

Adi smiled and wondered what reward Woodward would be giving him. Maybe he would get a position in the new administration and not have to live hand to mouth as a private investigator in the run-down parts of the city. He would soon know.

CHAPTER TWENTY-SIX

The tram system was of much higher quality than the one he was used to travelling on, and it was clear that security levels were high as Green Warriors were stopping the tram every few stops to check passengers. Even in this more refined atmosphere, Harry and his two android guardians were still attracting stares, and their passes provided by Sabella were double-checked every time by security.

Eventually, they reached Dore where they had been told to disembark and fought their way through the throngs of security forces and government workers to reach the security barriers where Sabella with some fierce-looking Green Warriors was waiting for them.

Sabella looked relieved that they had arrived and forced a smile as she greeted them. The red and black snake tattoo even seemed to be non-threatening but still seemed to be following Adi around with a fixed stare. Adi felt a sense of unease as he and Harry were escorted through security and a series of escalators, barriers, and well-lit corridors before they entered a large open square.

Adi looked up in amazement as the square seemed open to the elements and was surprised that they were not subject to the usual high temperatures of an ordinary day in Steel City. After close scrutiny, Adi realised that the sky was a *Trompe d'oeil* and was a fake representation of the outside world but designed to look real. Adi continued to marvel at the opulence of the surroundings with water fountains, statues, all dominated by a huge white sandstone building at the end of the square.

The Green Warriors escorted them all to the grand entrance of the Museum building where they handed them over to another group of Security staff. They had yellow stars on their uniforms which seemed to indicate they were of a higher status and allowed access to restricted areas. They were fast-tracked through a milling crowd and came to what looked like towering steps up to the top of the building. Once they stepped on to the first tread, everything started moving, and they were transported to the top of the building.

On reaching the final floor they found themselves in a circular room with numerous doors leading off to what appeared to be offices with different names on them. A couple of worker robots were removing these names and replacing them with new signs. Sabella led the way to what appeared to be the grandest of the entrances, and as they reached the threshold, Adi could see a gleaming new sign declaring that the occupant of the room was Woodward.

CHAPTER TWENTY-SEVEN

As they entered, Adi was struck by the wall to ceiling panoramic window with a view of the countryside away from Steel City. Woodward sat at an enormous shiny metallic desk and stood up as they all entered. Harry, who had until this point purposefully kept himself to the back of the group, propelled himself forward and hovered in front of Woodward. They both looked pleased as they greeted each other, as well as they were able and engaged in a hesitant mother/son embrace.

After a few seconds, Woodward appeared to pull herself together and realised that there were others in the room. She waved at Harry and pointed to a door through to some private quarters indicating that he and his two robots should go and wait for her there. A couple of Green Warriors escorted them to the room and stood guard by them once they had entered.

Woodward indicated to Sabella and Adi that they should sit down and she resumed sitting in her high-backed chair at her desk. The Green Warriors all moved away and stood guard at the only exit.

Woodward focused on a bemused Adi and looked him directly in the eye she said, "Firstly, Citizen Newton, congratulations and many thanks for your part in overthrowing the corrupt leaders who have exploited the people and resources of Steel City for far too long. Your help in tracking down my son, Harry, was invaluable, and both of your hacking skills made the elimination of the politburo members easier."

Adi looked relieved but wondered what plans Woodward had in mind for him. He hoped at least he could continue to work with Harry and wondered if they could be based in the more opulent area of Steel City.

Woodward looked at Adi and said, "Sabella and I owe you an explanation, Newton. Yes, we targeted you for your technical skills and knowledge of the dangerous areas of Steel City, but there was another reason. Before we get to that, let me update you what has happened and what we are planning to achieve."

Sabella took over the discussion, "You may know some of this, but probably you don't as the ruling elite like to keep the masses unaware and ignorant about who is in charge. The uncaring rulers for the last twenty years were the representatives of the Sino/Sovok bloc who took control of the parts of Europa that remained after the bulk of the mainland was made uninhabitable."

Woodward took up the narrative, "Angleterre, as it was called then, was ceded out as a colony of New Russia to the Sovoks. Following a succession of armed uprisings, many cities and towns were completely wiped off the map, and all that remained were the communities based around large metropolitan areas like Steel City."

Adi interjected, "But won't the Sino\Sovok bloc retaliate when they realise what you have done to eliminate their appointed rulers?"

Woodward gave Adi a condescending look and continued, "They have major problems and are glad to be rid of this one. Of the seven areas across the country, we are the fifth to revolt in such a manner, the other two will follow shortly. The Sovok Republic and Cathay are ravaged by internal disputes and the onset of a new lethal virus that is decimating their populations. We have taken back our City, and we are now in control."

Adi was taken aback at what he had been told, "Ok then, but who are 'we' and what are your plans?" He turned to face Sabella, "What is my role now in all this, you said it was vitally important I reached this meeting, why?"

Sabella glanced at Woodward, and they both seemed reluctant to speak. Adi spoke again, "Well come on, what next, I can't believe you haven't hatched a plan, do you want me do something for you in Dore, that would be better than having to go back to loppy Paradise."

Woodward took a deep breath, "Myself and Sabella along with others of a like mind are members of an underground organisation called 'Sceaf' which is what Steel City was called when it was founded many thousands of years ago. We seek to restore the values and beliefs of those times and follow the teachings of Alexandra de Lovelot. We have built alliances and planned for this day for many years and have established a loyal group of supporters, The Green Warriors."

Sabella took up the narrative, "We will be reversing many of the laws and customs imposed by the Sovoks, children will be brought up in families again and not indoctrinated and conditioned in state-run nurseries. We will seek to improve the living conditions of those living in the outlying areas, and we will incorporate those with a disability into our society, useful citizens like Harry, Woodward's son."

Woodward took over again, "You may also have realised by now that women will be in charge, we have had enough of corrupt male leaders exploiting society, particularly females and children. We also have strict customs and practices that we have to follow and will be organising celebratory events to mark our takeover of Steel City or Sceaf as it will be now known. We have to destroy all traces and links to the previous regimes and will mark the changeover with a ritual ceremony that will be compulsory newscast to all citizens."

Sabella looked closely at a now confused Adi, "We have already eliminated all the Sovok representatives and put our people in their positions of power. The remaining militia has accepted that we are now in control and all levels of the police are with us. Thanks to your information we have made contact with the main enforcers of the criminal groups in Paradise and other outlying areas, and they now know they have to work with us. The ritual ceremony will also emphasize that all citizens will need to co-operate. The alternative is elimination."

Adi was beginning to have a foreboding feeling and sweat was trickling down his spine, "But what the fuck has this to do with me?"

Woodward let out a deep sigh, "We are deeply sorry about this Citizen Newton, but we need to explain the difficult position we, and you are in. We need someone connected or related to one of the Sovok elite for our ceremony to highlight driving out the old and celebrating the new. I will allow Sabella to explain."

Sabella was unable to look Adi in the eye and started talking in a low voice, "Sorry boy, but will explain. When we put you into that deep coma so that we could trace your buried memories of the abuse you suffered at Hawking College, we also made an inadvertent but important discovery about your parents. Your mother was a cleaning operative here in Dore Village, but it is apparent that your father was the first Commander of the Sovok invaders just after they arrived in Steel City. His name was Yuri Sorokin, and he was your father. Sorokin was a feared and ruthless dictator responsible for executing many citizens of Steel City, including, it appears your birth mother."

Woodward with a new steely determination in her voice, "I am sorry Citizen Newton, but you have to make the ultimate sacrifice for Steel City." Sabella motioned to the Green Warrior guards by the door, and they moved towards Adi, and before he knew it, he was trussed up with electronic handcuffs.

Sabella spoke to the guards, "Citizen Newton needs to be taken to The Killing Field for the sacrificial ceremony, please hurry as the planned transmission is within a couple of hours." Sabella then squeezed Adi's hand and whispered to him, "Sorry it had to be this way, but I have given instructions that they will pump you full of pain killers to alleviate some of the distress, bless you, Newton."

Woodward turned to Sabella, "We need to start allocating offices and living quarters, let's get it sorted before the ceremony."

Adi was taken out of the room by the Green Warriors, and they started on their journey to The Killing Field. Adi glanced at one of the windows and saw Harry and Sioux watching. Adi tried to manipulate his hand so that he could reach into his inside pocket to grab something that could help his escape, but all he managed to do was turn on his music system.

It was The Who with *Won't Get Fooled Again*.

GLOSSARY

Dorogoy: Dear

Loppy: Dirty (Sheffield slang)

Maskirovka: is a military doctrine that covers a broad range of measures for military deception, from camouflage to denial and deception

Matryoshka: The Matryoshka doll is a symbol of the Russian babushka, a strong female matriarch and a central figure in the Russian family

Miy Druh: My Friend

Nomenklatura: were the people the Sovok Party *approved* of and *appointed* to positions of authority.

Rabochiye: Workers

Udachi: Good Luck

Jennel: Sheffield slang for 'alleyway.' Variations include: *gennel* or *ginnel*

The numbers, times, dates and measurements are generally Russian and easy to look up. Enjoy.

DISKOGRAPHY

The Hacker (1988)

Buried Dreams (1989)

Clock DVA:

Knife Slits Water (1982)

A Certain Ratio

Touch Sensitivity (1980)

Seventh Heaven (1980)

De Tian:

Kebab-Träume (1980)

Deutsch Amerikanische Freundschaft

Corrective Treatment (c. 1979)

Repression (c. 1979)

Disease

Waltz for Aidan

May Nothing But Happiness Enter Your Door

(1999, from album *Come On Die Young*)

Mogwai

Death's Doll

Fix Your Face

(1977, from Album Molodoy)

Molodoy

One Step More and You Die (2002 Album)

Mono

Barbarism Begins at Home (1985)

The Smiths

Beautiful People (1980)

Stunt Kites

Genetic Warfare (1979)

Vice Versa

Please find and play these wonderful tracks.